MECHANICS·
MERCANTILE
LIBRARY.

Arthur F. Mathews '06

TONGUE

# TONGUE

A Novel

KYUNG RAN JO

Translated by
CHI-YOUNG KIM

BLOOMSBURY

New York   Berlin   London

Published by Bloomsbury USA, New York

All papers used by Bloomsbury USA are natural, recyclable
products made from wood grown in well-managed forests.
The manufacturing processes conform to the environmental
regulations of the country of origin.

LIBRARY OF CONGRESS CATALOGING-IN-PUBLICATION DATA

Jo, Kyung Ran.
[Hyeo. English]
Tongue : a novel / Kyung Ran Jo; translated by Chi-Young Kim.—1st U.S. ed.
p. cm.
ISBN-13: 978-1-59691-651-7 (pbk.)
ISBN-10: 1-59691-651-6 (pbk.)
1. Women cooks—Fiction. 2. Self-realization in women—Fiction.
3. Cookery—Fiction. 4. Psychological fiction. I. Kim, Chi-Young. II. Title.

PL994.35.K98H94 2009
895.7'35—dc22
2008055743

First published in South Korea as *Hyeo* by
Munhakdongne Publishing Corp. in 2007
First U.S. Edition 2009

1 3 5 7 9 10 8 6 4 2

Typeset by Westchester Book Group
Printed in the United States of America by Quebecor World Fairfield

# CONTENTS

# JANUARY

*The surface on which you work (preferably marble), the tools, the ingredients, and your fingers should be chilled throughout the operation . . .*

—The Joy of Cooking

# CHAPTER 1

L ARGE PUPILS, TINTED CHARCOAL and light brown. My eyes once gleamed of strong resolve, shined with tense sensuality. I can't stand these eyes—weepy eyes reflected on the bottom of the copper pot, eyes expecting something from someone despite the knowledge that disappointment will be the result. *Please don't cry, I can't cry.* I close my eyes, open them. Now it's all right. I flip over the pot and hang it on its hook. Thankfully my tears are gone. Now I will myself to reach over to the rotating shelf where I keep various oils, select the bottle of extra-virgin olive oil, and turn toward the nine students who have gathered here at seven P.M., their clothes slightly rumpled from the day.

Gathered here at Won's Kitchen, which is outfitted with a ceramic stone pizza oven, refrigerator, dishwasher, coffeemaker, blender, mixer, food processor, electric rice cooker, gas stove. Assorted copper pots and stainless-steel pans hang from the ceiling in order of size, from large to medium to small. Along with glasses, a ventilation fan, food-waste compressor, electric grill,

3

shelves, vent hood, heating station, island, backless stools, and a pot of vigorously boiling water.

Grandmother always had a large table in her kitchen. The family gathered around the rectangular wooden table, as simple and unadorned as a desk, and when night fell each went his way. Even after she moved to the city, Grandmother always kept a bamboo basket of fruit or vegetables in the middle of the table. By leaving ingredients where she could see them, she was inspired to make new dishes every time she passed by the table. Sometimes the basket would hold warm, just-cooked yams or potatoes, white steam wafting up. Grandmother was the best cook I knew, but she didn't do much to yams, potatoes, or pumpkins other than steam or bake them. She could have sprinkled cheese over them while piping hot or added broth to make soup or purée, but didn't. Grandmother would say these things are supposed to be eaten plain, because you're eating the earth. By the time I realized that Grandmother's words symbolized her life, her simple, beautiful life, she was no longer with us. Morning sunlight streamed through her east-facing kitchen windows, rippling through the pear and apple blossoms outside, and I would shield my eyes from the sun and slurp up soup of shepherd's purse.

Beep. It's the oven timer.

I top the dough with sun-dried tomatoes, thick slices of mushrooms, basil leaves, and mozzarella rounds, sprinkle two tablespoons of olive oil over it all, and slide it into the preheated oven. It bakes for fifteen minutes until the cheese melts, the crust browning nicely, and then we have today's dish, sun-dried-tomato-and-mushroom pizza. Today I don't think I can make little snacks to share with the students or talk about the weather just like it's any other day—until the pizza's done. I explain to the students how to dry tomatoes at home using their ovens. Sun-dried tomatoes have a more intense flavor and scent than

4

fresh ones, but they're an expensive specialty food. I still have ten minutes. I reach into the basket in front of me and hold up whatever my hand closes around first. An apple.

"Variety and spontaneity are two of the most important things to keep in mind when you cook."

Everyone focuses on the apple I'm holding at eye level. In the Middle Ages, monks believed that this fruit contained the will of the Creator. The apple was said to taste of nature, of mystery, of the shapes of clouds and of the sound of wind rustling the leaves on trees, but the monks forbade its consumption. All because of the sweetness that filled your mouth when you took the first bite. They believed this sweetness was a temptation, one that would get in the way of concentrating on God's words. And after the sweetness dissipated, a tart, acidic zing lingered on the tip of your tongue. The monks thought this was the taste of poison, of the devil himself. This sweet, sour, tart taste of an apple—it's this taste Eve found irresistible.

"If you don't like mushrooms, you can use an apple instead. Slice an apple into pieces about five millimeters thick. You'll be able to experience something different, in contrast to the mushroom's light blandness. It's a little sweet, but the crunch can be very refreshing." I wish I'd picked up an eggplant instead. I've never tried substituting an apple for mushrooms in a pizza. Lies. Was it his lies I'd wanted? The first taste of an apple, the serpent's words—as sweet as honey. The second taste, banishment from the Garden of Eden—tart. Unlike other fruits that are soft when ripe, an apple should be firm. I slip the small paring knife from the knife block, the crowded home to twelve knives. Instead of cutting the apple crosswise, I slide my knife into it at a slant, creating a V shape, carving out an indent, and pop the piece into my mouth.

It's my first kitchen. In the beginning, I had everything in this kitchen, just like Grandmother's. Sunlight and plants and a clock

5

and newspapers and mail and fruit and vegetables, milk and cheese and bread and butter, tall glass bottles filled with fruit-infused liquor and smaller bottles of spices, the homey smell of simmering rice and the aroma of herbs. And two people.

When we started looking for spaces that could be home to a larger kitchen for our cooking classes, I insisted on a wall of large windows. I didn't consider basement locations even if they were huge and the lease was dirt cheap. My desire for windows must have come from memories of Grandmother's kitchen. I believed that everything came in through the kitchen, and for that we needed to have tall windows that would guarantee good light. Even when I traveled I always looked for restaurants that opened onto the street. He was the one who found the two-story building rich with windows. My excitement reached new heights even before we finished renovating the kitchen to make it roomier. This was only three years ago.

Grandmother was right. Just having a state-of-the-art kitchen doesn't make the food taste better or the cook happier. The most important thing in a kitchen isn't how delectable the food is but how happy you are while you're there. And you always have to leave the kitchen in that contented state. When I was young I would bolt into the kitchen as soon as I got home, but right now I find myself backing out of it just as rapidly, as if an unknown force is yanking me out.

Startled by the second buzz of the timer, I drop the apple to the floor. A drop of off-white juice splashes on my calf. I'm rooted in place, watching—Paulie, who's been lying quietly under the table, grips the apple with his teeth and scurries out. The V mark on the apple's red peel looks like a stain that can't be removed even with bleach. If you cut an apple in half, you'll discover five seeds as big as a watermelon's, studded in a star shape in the middle of the round surface. Is it that I want to continue thinking that an apple isn't just an apple, that it's a secret sign only I can see? I pull the crispy, well-baked pizza out of the oven, thinking, I've come so far—too far. I close my eyes, open them. I open my mouth to say, "This is the last class."

I've read so many books where the story starts with a man meeting a woman, and then they fall in love. But my story begins with love's demise. I used to read Hemingway for the simple reason of his being a gourmet. What Hemingway said is wrong—it isn't only men who discover themselves after experiencing physical pain.

# CHAPTER 2

DESCENDING DUSK AND COLD WEATHER and heavy snows and gusty wind—back when this was what January meant, I didn't actually know anything about the weather outside or the drifts of snow or wind. I was always behind windows, cradling in my hands a steaming cup of French-pressed coffee or a mug of cognac-enhanced hot chocolate. I would watch the heavy snow coming down in the late afternoon, dip a piece of warm buttered baguette in my hot chocolate, take a bite, and exclaim, Wow, there's so much snow! And that would be it. Hot and sweet—that was January. Heat and sweetness were also the first sensations to go.

I can't taste the bitter and full-bodied French Valrhona chocolate or the flavorful bite of the cognac. My entire body is tense, the way it is when I have to open my mouth for the first time in front of a man. I swallow a mouthful of freshly made hot chocolate, the liquid coating my throat. The snow is letting up and slender rays of light slice through the dark clouds. But the inside of my mouth remains numb. I ask myself, is this drink hot? Or cold? That feels as meaningless as if I'm asking myself whether I'm hot or cold. The state of being neither hot nor cold—this is the first step toward the path of rage and fear.

Only four genes control vision, but more than one thousand genes are involved with smell and taste. But one thousand genes can disappear faster than the four. I've already lost two things—this kitchen and the taste for sweet, hot liquid. I may lose everything I have, but I want to be able to keep just two things. It doesn't feel odd that he isn't one of them. I know of people who chose death when they lost their taste buds. I need a kitchen even if it isn't this one, and it's crucial that I keep working.

I push the now-cold mug onto the table, casting it away. I have to think about what I can do right now. And about how I can emerge from this funk. I swallow, thinking of the freshness of a winter carrot and the spirited crunch of a radish. Some people like to eat anything soft and pliant, or food that bursts in their mouths when they bite into it. Some enjoy meat juices slowly seeping into the spaces between their teeth, and others like to crunch on plain raw vegetables. I can't live without vegetables. When I think of raw carrot salad—a fresh carrot just pulled from the ground with leafy green fronds still waving from its top, julienned, dressed with olive oil, minced garlic, lemon juice, salt, ground black pepper, chilled in the fridge for about four hours, then sprinkled with chopped parsley right before you dig in—I can feel saliva pooling slowly from the back of my mouth. His favorite dish is steak, rare and tender and moist, seared just enough to elevate it from its primal rawness, with a side of baked potato. It's the first dish I made him. The carrot, the sweet, cold carrot salad, as refreshing as crunching down on a cube of ice—I'm okay, for now.

Restaurant Nove. In Italian, it means the number nine. It's the only restaurant I've cooked at. I didn't know I would be back here. When I first started working here at the age of twenty, I named the persimmon tree outside the two-story building Caper, because the persimmons dangling from the branches in the fall looked just like the flower buds of capers on the cusp of blooming. I slowly climb the stairs and look through the floor-to-ceiling glass of the restaurant. There must be something that's different, but everything seems the same— closing at this time of day to prepare for dinner service, setting the table with light-gray linens instead of white from September to February, and Chef sitting at a table by the window, staring outside or scratching away on his pad with his head bowed, coming up with a new menu. If only I could open that door and walk in as if nothing had happened. Then would I believe I'm happy? I ask Chef in my head, the glass window between us.

Chef is a big man, with especially brawny shoulders and a back like a kendo player, but a little bent over. If he were an animal he would be a bull, with intense eyes and his entire body radiating power. A bull—one that doesn't compromise and moves with determination and is brave. If he were a fish, he would obviously be a large, thick, saw-edged perch that weighs over forty kilograms, the carnivorous fish that keeps to itself. The first time I met him, he was slouched at a white-tableclothed table, smoking a cigar as leisurely as if he were merely the owner, not the chef. Back then, he tied his long hair back in a ponytail. Now his graying hair is buzzed like that of a soldier. I'm relieved—it must not only be children who are reassured when surrounded by familiar sights. Like a cook who'd gone on break after lunch service and was returning for dinner service after changing into clean whites, I pull open the heavy glass doors and burst in.

Chef looks up, surprised.

"Can I have some tea too?" I nod at the large white porcelain café au lait cup in front of Chef and sit down. This would be easier if he asked why I'm here, but Chef doesn't say a word.

"I just came by to have some tea," I continue.

"What?"

"Huh?"

"Do you have something to say to me?"

I don't say anything.

"It's almost time for dinner service."

"I want to work again."

"Where?"

"Here."

"You said nothing was going on."

"Nothing's going on." Chef has known me for thirteen years, since I was twenty. It's impossible to lie to his face, sitting here across from him.

"So what's the matter?"

I can't say anything.

"What about the cooking classes?"

"I'm wrapping them up."

He stands and stalks into the kitchen, annoyed. The kitchen isn't a place just anyone can walk into, not even me. The pass dividing the dining room and the kitchen isn't long, but the two areas are completely different in character and purpose—people waiting for food and people making it, people being waited on and people serving them. Right now I'm not waiting for food or making it, nor am I being waited on or serving someone, and the distance between the kitchen and the dining room feels vast. It's hot in here, even though the snow on the ground outside is starting to freeze. I look around in a manner that might make an observer think I'm bored.

Three years ago they took down the wall between the kitchen and the dining room to create a more airy interior, but when I worked here, the kitchen was as stuffy as a preheated four-

12

hundred-degree oven. If you stood in the kitchen for five hours, where the window was closed even in the middle of summer to keep the food hot, the threads of your uniform melted and stuck to your skin. Nobody said things like It's too hot in here. Even big restaurants don't have spacious kitchens, because you have to save space in order to squeeze in another table.

If nothing has changed since my days here, I can still tell you everything about the place, even the number of glasses lined up in the kitchen right now. But something has definitely shifted, just like the way I couldn't brazenly follow Chef into the kitchen. Now, for me, the kitchen is no longer solely the place that delicious food comes from.

Chef reappears and sits across the table, pushing a large porcelain cup in front of me. I blow on the tea to cool it and touch my lips to the edge of the cup. Bitter and nutty and sour and sharp—tea with coffee, milk, and ground dried chicory. When I worked here, I always made myself a cup of this tea in the middle of the afternoon.

"I don't know whether I should say this . . ." Chef said.

"Go ahead."

"This kind of desperation—"

I don't want to hear that mine is a desperate love.

"—is always hard to get through."

In a situation like this, it's uncomfortable to talk to someone who's older. Chef's tone is that of a person who's lived his entire life according to his convictions and beliefs. Afraid that his voice will grab me by the throat and shake me as if with a big hand, I quickly ask, "So I can start tomorrow, right?"

All I'm here to do is to find work. Nobody is allowed to say that my relationship is over, not yet. I suppress the urge to slink quietly out the back door and force myself to watch his eyes. *The thing more terrifying than splitting up with him is that I'm*

13

*still with him in my heart even though we're not together anymore. I mean, maybe it's a test—if you want to know someone, if you really want to know someone, you have to try a separation, maybe just once, just this one time. Please don't ask me about it right now.*

"So you still have that habit of staring someone in the eyes," Chef says.

"I haven't changed at all."

"There's something that's different."

I don't say anything.

"End it while you still can. Stop dragging your feet. It'll be much easier after some time passes."

"I guess it'll get better by the time it's peak croaker season." Summer. At 5:05 P.M. on January 20, the midwinter point according to the traditional Chinese calendar and supposedly the coldest day of the year, I am talking out of the blue about summer. Chef gets up, grunting from the exertion. The kitchen is at its busiest at this time.

"Eat something before you go," Chef suggests.

"Don't you have a lot of covers?"

"Then go."

"No, no, I'm hungry. What's good today?"

"Sea bass."

"Okay, then I'll have some sea bass."

14

# CHAPTER 3

W HEN I SEE a house whose living room is brightly lit in
the middle of the night, I think of two possibilities. Two
people sitting across from each other, swirling glasses of wine, lit
by subtly scented candles. Or two people fighting, arguing like it
will never end. People don't have spats in the dark. In the dark
people make love or talk. The far superior option is to eat as you
talk. Anyway, it's not a good sign that the lights are on in our
house late into the night. The thing I want to do most right now
isn't make love or talk or cook. I want to walk around the whole
house, barefoot, and slowly switch off all the lights. Usually at
this time, I'm in the bedroom or in the kitchen with the lights
dimmed, making a simple late-night snack. But right now I'm
not doing either. I can't believe all the lights are on at one in the
morning, like at a hatchery. I watch him as he walks around the
house, unrushed, packing his things.

He used to say, At night, I sit on the sofa like this and think
about the happiest moment of my day. Then I get up slowly,
turn out every light in the house, and go into the bedroom calm

15

and relaxed. I close the door gently. I pull back the sheets and lie in bed, and I can smell the dried lavender from my pillow. The most important thing is that you're always lying there next to me.

Once a friend said that falling in love is like carving a word on the back of your hand. Even if you rub it out as hard as you can, a faint residue is left behind. So you have to be certain that you really want it. Make sure you think about it.

Even though she'd never met him, my friend talked about him a lot. No, I talked about him a lot and she must have been listening. And she remembered everything I said. *You're right. I need to be certain about it right now, certain that this isn't the end—it can't be over like this.*

"Come here, Paulie!" he calls.

Paulie, who was hunched by my feet, glances up at me, gets up slowly, and pads over to him. By now Paulie and I both know what this means. It means that he has something to say to me. I'm not sure when it started, but he calls Paulie's name instead of mine. I caress the cutting board with one hand and walk into the living room.

"I'm going to have people come and pack up that painting. I'll tell them to call to make sure you're home. I took care of all of our accounts at the bank, too. There shouldn't be anything that you have to manage by yourself. I'll call if I've forgotten something . . . I don't really know how we're supposed to deal with something like this. I'm going to Dubai for work in a week. I'll be there for about two weeks. I don't think I can leave the key, though, because I have to come see Paulie." He clamps his mouth suddenly, as if he's uncomfortable. If we'd had a child, would he have said he'd come by to see the kid like that? I don't know what the end of a relationship is supposed to be like either—do I hurry up and say what I need to say as if I'm being chased, just as he's doing, or do I cry and buy some time?

16

"Do you want something to eat?" I ask, studying his sallow face.

"Huh. You're so unemotional." He leaks a smile.

It's not the most adequate thing to say to someone who's walking out on you, but I can't think of anything better. I wouldn't know of anything better to say anyway. Gogol wrote extensively about food, and was undoubtedly obsessed with it. The couples in his stories always express their love by feeding each other smoked sturgeon, fruit jelly, sausage, pancakes, mushrooms, melons. One couple eats eleven-course meals daily. One day, the husband suggests to his dying wife, "Perhaps you would eat a little something." After she dies, he sheds tears at the sight of her favorite dishes. The man ends up starving himself to death. I wish someone would suggest the same thing to me right now: Perhaps you would eat a little something. I would probably say that to him when he's on his deathbed, urging, It's not too late, just ask for it and I'll make it for you. What about a slab of rare steak like that first time?

I remember the day he came into the restaurant to look for me. Cooks rarely come out of the kitchen. Even Chef never goes into the dining room during service unless someone he knows comes to the restaurant. Chef doesn't trust cooks who meddle in the affairs of the dining room and sternly prohibited me from doing so. That evening was the first time I went onto the floor during dinner service. Manager Park, clad in a stylish white shirt and black vest, called me in—*Ji-won, a customer came in with your business card. He wants you to make him this dish. Do you know him?* Oh, okay, I replied, but I wondered who it was. I glimpsed the person's face, the one who'd come in with my business card and ordered steak. I stared at him like I had the first time I saw him.

Yes. It was him. I had met him at a pizzeria in Napoli, where I had worked for ten days for no pay to learn how to make pizza. My face flushed. It had been one month since I'd returned to Seoul. And here he was, thirty days after our first meeting.

I went back to the grill station to sear the herb-marinated beef and cut a cross into the top of a potato to stick it in the oven. Sweat rolled off my face. The tiramisu I'd made in the morning had come out exceptionally well, and I'd taken a thirty-minute nap in the afternoon. And he had come here in the evening. When I go to bed later, I may be in an even better mood, I thought, as if chanting a spell. It wouldn't do if I thought about something sad or if I were stressed, because those emotions could seep into my cooking. I laughed out loud. I turned over the steak. It's going to be fantastic, I said, loud enough for the potato to hear me. I filled the opening of the potato with crème fraîche. I slid my knife under the beef and moved it from the grill, plating it in the center of the platter. I added some mustard sauce as well as some roasted asparagus, which usually wasn't part of the dish. It was done. I placed the platter on the pass. Which wine did he order? I asked Manager Park. Barolo Zonchera, he replied. A solid choice. Manager Park lifted the platter easily and headed toward his table. I supported myself on the pass with both arms, my upper body sticking out. I could see him unfold the napkin onto his lap and slowly pick up his fork and knife.

It looked as if he was poking at the middle of the steak with his knife. I tensed. A satisfied smile bloomed on his lips. The meat was perfectly cooked, offering just the right amount of resistance before giving way to the knife. Go ahead, take a bite, I said quietly from behind the pass. He cut off a piece and put it into his mouth and chewed. He nodded once, as if to say, Not bad at all, and cut another piece. I stood there until he was done, not missing a single moment, even seeing his lips plump with pleasure. When you eat, all the blood rushes to your lips, which become red and puffy. Like the penis when making love. Lips and penises and tongues are all special erogenous zones, crowded with nerve endings. The most sensitive moment for the tongue is the exact instant it's touched by food.

He drank some water, then took a sip of wine. He cut into his steak and chewed, savoring it. He had a good appetite. As Uncle had told me bitterly, you can't continue a relationship with people who don't want to eat anything, no matter how much you love them. If someone has a good appetite, there will be room for you to be included. He cut another piece and ate it with gusto. I didn't miss a single second of it. I stared at him so intently that I was eating that steak myself. He was cutting into me, putting me into his mouth, chewing me. I felt my lips swell like well-ripened plum tomatoes, red and taut. Next time I'll make you a dish with truffles, I said, gently wiping my mouth with the back of my hand. Truffles and asparagus are some of my favorites, both sprouting from the depths of the earth. I believed that's how love grew as well.

"It's too late to eat." His voice is no longer conciliatory or contrite. I nod lightly. Eating and loving—impossible for us right now, as they require us to have warmth in our bodies.

He's gripping the handle of the front door. "See you," he says, his eyes on Paulie. Paulie comes up behind me slowly and pushes his head lightly against the back of my knees. *Just smile at me once, even if it's awkward, just like the first time you saw me.* I watch him take a step outside and turn my back on him. If we had been a single line before, one line neatly on top of the other, now we are two separate lines going different ways. Two slanting lines are bound to meet somewhere. This feels like an obvious truth, like the way liquid always flows downward. That's why I can send him off like this. It will just take time for us.

I'll feel better if I eat something sweet, Paulie, I say. If there's no cake, alcohol isn't a bad substitute. I'm going to pour liquor to the rim of the glass, until it overflows, aggressively lick the edge of the glass, then down it. I'll gulp it in a split second, practically leaving an imprint of my teeth on the glass. Paulie barks. I hear the door close. Don't bark, Paulie! I throw open the refrigerator doors as if I am yanking drapes apart. Chilly air assaults me.

# CHAPTER 4

I F LONELINESS OR SADNESS or happiness could be expressed through food, loneliness would be basil. It's not good
for your stomach, dims your eyes, and turns your mind murky. If
you pound basil and place a stone over it, scorpions swarm toward it. Happiness is saffron, from the crocus that blooms in the
spring. Even if you add just a pinch to a dish, it adds an intense
taste and a lingering scent. You can find it anywhere but you
can't get it at any time of the year. It's good for your heart, and
if you drop a little bit in your wine, you instantly become drunk
from its heady perfume. The best saffron crumbles at the touch
and instantaneously emits its fragrance. Sadness is a knobby cucumber, whose aroma you can detect from far away. It's tough
and hard to digest and makes you fall ill with a high fever. It's
porous, excellent at absorption, and sponges up spices, guaranteeing a lengthy period of preservation. Pickles are the best food
you can make from cucumbers. You boil vinegar and pour it over
the cucumbers, then season with salt and pepper. You enclose

them in a sterilized glass jar, seal it, and store it in a dark and dry place.

WON'S KITCHEN. I take off the sign hanging by the first-floor entryway. He designed it by hand and silk-screened it onto a metal plate. Early in the morning on the day of the opening party for the cooking school, he had me hang the sign myself. I was meaning to give it a really special name, he said, grinning, flashing his white teeth, but I thought Jeong Ji-won was the most special name in the world. He called my name again: Hey, Ji-won.

He walked around the house calling my name over and over, mischievously—as if he were an Eskimo who believed that the soul became imprinted in the name when it was called—while I fried an egg, cautiously sprinkling grated Emmentaler, salt, pepper, taking care not to pop the yolk. I spread the white sun-dried tablecloth on the coffee table and set it with the fried egg, unsalted butter, blueberry jam, and a baguette I'd toasted in the oven. It was our favorite breakfast: simple, warm, sweet. As was his habit, he spread a thick layer of butter and jam on his baguette and dunked it into his coffee, and I plunked into my cup the teaspoon laced with jam, waiting for the sticky sweetness to melt into the hot, dark coffee.

I still remember the sugary jam infusing the last drop of coffee and the moist crumbs of the baguette lingering at the roof of my mouth. And also his words, informing me that he wanted to design a new house that would contain the cooking school, his office, and our bedroom. Instead of replying, I picked up a firm red radish, sparkling with droplets of water, dabbed a little butter on it, dipped it in salt, and stuck it into my mouth. A crunch resonated from my mouth. Hoping the crunch sounded like, Yes, someday, I continued to eat it. Was that the reason I equated a fresh red radish with sprouting green tops, as small as a miniature apple, with the taste of love? But if I cut into it crosswise like an apple, I wouldn't find the constellation of seeds.

Once I take down the sign I'm unmoored, as though I have nothing else to do, as if my name were forever erased from the world.

After he's gone I curl up on the couch in the living room, immobile. I lie there quietly, sensing the wind blowing outside, the setting sun, the arrival of morning, the descent of cold, my throat starting to hurt. I don't fry an egg or toast bread. I heave myself from the couch once in a while to take a sip of water, and when it feels like the long, sharp end of a dried-up, hard-as-rock baguette is jabbing into my forehead, I make a face and manage to pour hot water into the coffee press for a cup. Right now, in this house, the only things I can keep down seem to be water, coffee, air. I quit counting the days after the third day. I'm gradually being split into pieces—my shoulders and arms, my head and neck. When I realize it's night again, I feel faint, as if my tired body is laid in a large, hot copper pan. Am I slowly disappearing without attracting any attention, like a small dot? I want to stir, to move and feel my fingers and toes that seem to be evaporating, but I can't. Help, help me up, I whisper into the deep, dark green of night. You have to snap out of this, Uncle says. You can't allow yourself to wallow in a pool of sorrow. Get up!

Something large and hot and wet sweeps across my cheek.

I open my eyes.

Paulie is licking my face. His wide, black pupils are staring at me quietly.

Did . . . someone come by? I ask, raising my upper body.

Paulie barks once, in a low tone. He lies down quietly, twice shaking his head so that his ears, drooping and folded backward, swing to the front of his head. It's his way of saying he's hungry. I slide my hand under Paulie's belly and pet his soft, silky coat. English setters—famous for being an elegant, powerful, expressive breed, lying quietly at their owners' feet, pointing at prey without barking—are no longer valued for their hunting prowess. Instead they are prized for the long, silky, beautiful light-brown fur draping their bodies and their aristocratic beauty, which reveals itself when they prance around slowly, shaking their hair, taking a viewer's breath away. Paulie nudges my knee with his nose. He seems to be saying, You'll take care of me, right? Instead of agreeing, I rub his head with my palms—Paulie, such a loving, independent dog, with a weak homing instinct. He emits another low bark. Do you want to leave too? I ask him. Paulie flattens his stomach on the ground and puts his head on his front paws as if to say, I have to rest here a little.

Paulie is his dog. He trained him, saying, He reacts when I call his name, so maybe it's possible to teach Paulie actual words. With Paulie, he disliked using orders like sit, stand, go back, go forward, go away, don't bark, lie down, no, wait. Instead he wanted to teach words he could listen and react to, like Are you hungry? Do you want to go for a walk? Do you know that person? We discovered that, depending on the pitch, length, and frequency of Paulie's noises, there was an imperfect but workable sphere of communication between us. But just as dogs saw the world in grays, dark browns, and greens, there was a limit to the language we could converse in. This is good enough, he'd said, pleased. Now he's gone and left, giving me the dog he'd trained, the dog he'd raised for fifteen years, the dog he'd had even before he met me. Once the decision was made that we were to separate, we divided up our belongings as if we were playing jacks, but the problem of who would keep the dog was surprisingly easy. She didn't like dogs.

*We were rejected, you and me.* I want to kneel on the ground and lightly nudge Paulie with my nose, ask him, You're going to take care of me now, right? Something hot surges up from deep down within me. I swipe the back of my hand against my face, and then, because it feels as if I'm stuck in a tight corner, I touch my fingers, feet, and nose, carefully and seriously. The body parts that protrude, like noses and fingers, show the most wear and tear. Even though it isn't perfect, my body is still held together in the right places and my fingers and toes still move freely. If I go limp now, if I give in to the heavy weight of sorrow, my body would quiver anew from the fresh sensation of pain—just like a sudden drip of candle wax on skin—and from the thrill of pleasure, all the more irresistible once I'd discovered it.

I've never even dreamed of what rejection would feel like, and I know that I need to sense pain and understand the reason behind it and force my way out of it. My eyes are sparkling, reflected in the living-room window, and my skin tightens and my muscles tense the same as when I make a sumptuous dish. Like a cork bobbing on water, I resurface lightly. And to push away the fear that is poised to grip me at any moment, I address Paulie in an unnecessarily loud voice: Paulie, want to go for a walk?

# FEBRUARY

*In the quest for gold a man may be lukewarm; but salt every one desires to find, and deservedly so, since to it every kind of meat owes its savor.*

—Cassiodorus, A.D. 523

# CHAPTER 5

IT'S SO COLD on the last day of the Lunar New Year holiday
that I buy a light-green down jacket on my way home from
a walk. Every time I move, my body seems to rattle like bones
encased in a tin. I go to work wearing that jacket. I run up the
two flights to the restaurant, hurrying up the wooden steps
whose edges are crusted with frozen snow. I took these stairs
every day from the age of twenty to twenty-nine, when I quit
to open the cooking school. Now, at thirty-three, I wish I could
say that I'd briefly gone to a place nobody knows about before
returning home. Just like the big and small scars on my arms,
from flipping hot pans or splattering oil, ugly spots have in-
vaded some part of my body under this heavy jacket. I grab the
cold, frozen handle of the glass door with both hands. My
palms stick to the surface. Now I'm one of seven cooks here.
The door glides open after a screech of resistance, forbidding.
I draw in a deep breath. Bread is already baking in the kitchen.

The other cooks talk about me when I'm not around, just
enough for me to detect the hush when I get back to my station.

In the bustling morning kitchen, as we marinate meat, bake bread and pastries, wash arugula, I try to think of myself as someone else in that kitchen, let's say someone named K. K, a disciple of the head chef, graduated from Appennino, the culinary school specializing in Italian cuisine, and was immediately hired by Nove. For six years she was Chef's trusted right hand and oversaw the kitchen with him. Within a year of becoming sous chef, she left to open a private cooking school, and some of Nove's regulars took their business to Won's Kitchen. The popularity of K's cooking classes spread through word of mouth in the trendy Gangnam area, but by that time K had split up with the young architect she'd lived with for seven years. The woman he'd fallen in love with was O, the famous model. K, left behind with a dog, shuttered her cooking school and returned to Nove—K's life can be summed up in only a few sentences. Now that I think of it, I would talk about K behind her back, too, and that makes me feel better. At least K doesn't have the kind of life that nobody would care to talk about.

My rank is below that of Manager Park, who was the youngest cook when I quit, but I don't have to wash and prepare vegetables or devein shrimp or debone chicken. Refusing to care what the others think of me, I bake, boil, steam, sauté, fry, season, stew in the small kitchen, next to the other cooks who don't know everything about K's life. A gossip in the kitchen would whisper that when K first got back here she was cowed by the senior cooks, but now she commands the kitchen a little too overtly, as if to show everyone that her burning desire is to work in this kitchen. K's appearance here for the first time in four years is the kind of thing that nobody talks about but everyone takes note of. I don't say a word, as if I know nothing about K. You talk about your knife slicing open your finger or shoes that pinch your feet, but you don't talk about what's in your heart. When I spread open the well-ironed white linens to change tables after a busy lunch service, I wonder, where did K's life go wrong?

As I noticed when I first came back, the practice of closing the restaurant between three and five in the afternoon is still the same. During that time we prep for dinner service and one of the cooks makes a snack—a simple roll stuffed with avocado or flying-fish roe, or a tiny portion of noodles that could be finished with three swipes of chopsticks—and shares it with the others. Before, I usually made omelets with a sprinkle of sugar or fruit salad from leftover fruit, hand-squeezed orange juice, and honey. Snacks have to be either salty or sweet.

I'm leaning on the wall of the metal staircase that leads downstairs, at the end of the hall past the bathroom, when I hear someone's footsteps approach. It doesn't seem prudent to be caught standing around by myself yet, I think, as I dust off my hands and turn around to head back in. Chef is striding over from the far end of the hall like an angry man, with half of a thick baguette in his hand, and, without giving me the chance to refuse, shoves it quickly and forcefully into my mouth. "I don't need a cook who doesn't eat."

I'm caught off guard.

"Did you forget that you have to be physically fit for this job?"

I'm quiet.

"Say you'll eat it!"

I can't answer because the baguette has taken over my mouth. In the kitchen, I watch what Chef is cooking, listen carefully for the words he sometimes utters, get a whiff with my nose, and, instead of asking questions, sneak a taste when he's not there, just as I did back when I was an apprentice. So how did Chef figure out that I'm not eating anything? It's only been three days since I started work.

After spending all that time in bed, I realized I was treating the act of eating as though it's the art of Zen, taking in just

31

enough, a little at a time, slowly. Exactly the way I never did with food. Like dancing without passion, eating like that will never awaken your palate. K may have lost another crucial thing: the obsession with good food, the strong impulse to make and eat it. Chef is right. There's no need for a cook who doesn't eat—you don't only cook when you're holding a knife in the kitchen.

A heavy weight presses down on me, all the way down to my uvula. I nod, once. *Cold beef topped with a salad of mushrooms, pickle, onion, tomato, oh, and this is Camembert, and you've spread whole-seed mustard on the bread.* I gulp down the sandwich, watching Chef walk back into the kitchen. He rarely makes snacks himself, usually just grabbing a banana or an orange, sometimes downing a cup of coffee in place of a meal. You haven't changed a bit, I think as I swallow the sandwich he made for me. *And really, this is so big and delicious.*

# CHAPTER 6

I CATCH A GLIMPSE of Mun-ju walking up the stairs, wearing a dark chive-green coat. It's the first time I've seen her since she came to my place last month to make me porridge. I'm glad it's her. Ever since I've been back at Nove, people I know come in unexpectedly, order food, and call me to the table and pour me a glass of wine after the meal. Won's Kitchen must have been more famous than I'd realized. Avoiding their sympathetic glances that transmit *How are you? I know it must be hard*, I carefully empty the wineglass and send out dessert on the house, something like black-rice ice cream or lemon sherbet. When a cook sends out dessert on the house, something you didn't even order, it has one of two meanings—This is really delicious, please try it and marvel at my work, or Please get up from the table. These days when I send out dessert—its etymology being "clear the table"—the latter is what I'm trying to convey. There's a saying: You don't give sour fruit to a sick person.

Mun-ju, who's holding the menu like a book, orders onion soup and abalone risotto in a tone of voice that indicates, I don't have an appetite, but I guess I should get something, right? and pushes the menu away. She still doesn't meet my eyes.

I say, "It's after nine thirty. The kitchen's closed."

"Well, good. Now that I see you, I don't want to eat anything."

"Why not?"

"What is this? You look like you're starving."

I leak a smile despite myself—even though I've lost weight, it can't be that bad. I go back into the kitchen, entrust her order to Choi, the most junior prep cook, and bring out a basket of herb-and-garlic bread baked earlier this morning. Mun-ju likes to eat more bread than the actual meal and prefers nonalcoholic drinks like tea, coffee, or cocoa to liquor. Even at Won's Kitchen, she attended only the Bread and Cooking class that I conducted on the weekends. A basket brimming with warm bread is the most effective cure for the hungry, the dissatisfied, or the worried.

Mun-ju and I are still avoiding each other's gazes, pressing down on the crust with our fingertips or brushing off the crumbs in front of our bread plates with our palms. I wish I could just say it's all history. I want to tell her she shouldn't blame herself for everything that's happened to me. Because it really isn't her fault.

I met Mun-ju the day a magazine was supposed to come to the restaurant for a shoot. It was a food magazine, and there was a column in which leading French, Italian, and Korean restaurants presented a recipe made with the ingredient of the month, spinach. At Nove, the most famous dish was Chef's roasted duck breast topped with roots of baby spinach. I was shucking oysters for dinner service when Chef popped in and said, Why don't you try your hand at it? and left. It was one hour before the shoot. I was nervous even though it wasn't a special guest coming for a tasting—it was only a picture. It could have been Chef's way of testing me, Chef who taught me everything

I know, everything down to how to hold a knife. This might have been the chance to show him that I not only understood the recipe, but also his—my mentor's—palate. The inside of my mouth was practically burning with my desperate eagerness to make a roasted duck breast topped with roots of baby spinach that Chef would approve of, one that wouldn't merely look good for a picture but would make you salivate by just looking at it. I started to wash my hands but paused to pop a shucked, slippery, wet oyster into my mouth.

Spinach, with its brilliant color and subtle fragrance, goes well in vegetable dishes, but it's primarily used in meat dishes because of its vividness. Only two people I know use the entire vegetable, including the roots—Grandmother and Chef. When I parboiled spinach in salted water, squeezed out excess moisture, melted butter in a pan, sautéed the spinach on low heat, added salt, pepper, raisins, and plated it, Grandmother would say, You've made a snooty dish! And she'd eat it happily. But spinach is best the way Grandmother made it, parboiled in salted water and seasoned with garlic, salt, and sesame oil, using your hands. Chef removes only the outer leaves and the rough parts of the roots, doesn't cut it, and puts the whole thing into a steamer for a light steam. He seasons it only with a sprinkling of coarse sea salt, and the leaves are refreshing and the roots taste a little piquant. Its crunch goes well with the duck breast, marinated in the juices of pressed spinach, seared on the grill over high heat. The lasting flavor isn't the overpowering taste of a large cut of meat but the snap and sharpness of the baby spinach root. But if you're used to sweetness, it's hard to enjoy the bland and light taste of the spinach.

I carefully carried the large white oval plate with the roasted duck breast topped with baby spinach roots like it was a precious pot and put it on the table where the photographer and reporter were sitting—the reporter wearing a short bob with straight bangs, large gold rings dangling from her ears. Of all the tables by the window, it was the table that received the best natural light. Even without additional light, the brown duck and the light-green spinach would look brilliant.

I waited behind the restaurant, leaning on the metal staircase, facing the entrance. I saw the reporter and the photographer push through the glass doors and go down the stairs much earlier than I'd expected. I went inside, bewildered. The white plate was sitting on the table by the window like a still life, its contents untouched. I ran out the door and down the stairs.

"Wait!" I sprinted up to their car, which hadn't yet left the parking lot, and tapped the car door with my palm. The photographer, who was loading his equipment in the trunk, stuck his head out to see what was going on.

"Look!"

The reporter lowered the window from the passenger side. She looked up at me, eyes questioning.

"You can't just take a picture and leave!"

"What?"

"How can you write an article without tasting the food?" I protested, as if I were about to fling open the door and drag her out.

She got out unwillingly and asked me sharply, "So you're saying I have to eat it? Right now?"

I didn't answer. I hadn't planned on doing this. But if I cooked something and nobody ate it, I read that to mean they were contemptuous of me. And I'd only met this woman today. I turned around, disappointed.

"Oh, wait, you're totally serious?" She grabbed my arm and looked me in the eyes. She burst out in sudden laughter.

That was Yeo Mun-ju, my friend sitting across the table right now. *Cooking and Wine,* the magazine where Mun-ju worked, was the first magazine to run a feature on my food. Later, she was the one who suggested I open a cooking school.

"Did you meet your deadline?" I ask.

"Not yet. I think I will tomorrow."

"You must be tired. Eat, eat."

Mun-ju reluctantly dabs a piece of bread in oil and puts it into her mouth. I'd forgotten that it's the busiest time of the month for her. The magazine is only a five-minute walk from the restaurant. After that first shoot, their deadlines met, Mun-ju brought a horde of her coworkers even after the kitchen was closed, asking me to make some pasta or cold mixed noodles. I gladly cooked for her and her coworkers and uncorked the wine. It was before we'd become close, when the air between us was filled with curious and nervous tension, the days before we turned thirty.

I feel Mun-ju staring at my forehead.

"I told you that you should take some time off until spring before starting work again. You look so drained."

When I told her I was going back to work at Nove, Mun-ju wasn't too happy about it. She wanted us to take a trip together, even somewhere close, but I didn't want to. I didn't want to go anywhere. Now I feel most relieved and carefree when I'm in the kitchen. What I need now isn't rest, but labor.

"In the old days, farmed vegetables like radishes and carrots pulled themselves out of the ground in the early morning. They'd go in front of the farmer's house and stand in a single line, waiting for the farmer to pick what he needed. But one day the farmer was so hungover that he couldn't get out of bed, so he asked the vegetables to come back tomorrow. When this kept happening, the angry vegetables notified the farmer, Now we're just going to stay rooted underground. When you need something, you come and pull it out."

"That's not even remotely funny."

"They say that was the beginning of labor."

"So then you must know how the idea of rest came about?" Mun-ju retorts, in no mood to laugh over my story.

"I need to work like this so I can do things in the spring that can only be done then." I clasp my fingers together and stretch them over my head as if I'm planning to climb the mountains in the spring to pick wild rocambole and fatsia shoots and aster.

"Just push it out of your mind. I mean, what can you do at this point? At least you guys never got married. At least he has a conscience, leaving you that house without any hassle."

It wasn't without any hassle, but, as Mun-ju says, it wasn't as if we were married. But there's something I can't give up, something that isn't the house or the bank accounts.

"Mun-ju."

"Yeah?"

"I'm fine."

"Okay."

"Really."

"Okay. You're fine."

I am suddenly ravenous, even though it's after eleven P.M. I want to slice into a thick steak, seasoned with only salt and pepper.

# CHAPTER 7

T HE LAST THING Uncle gave me before he left was a half-transparent rock the size of a man's fist. I studied the rock, the surface of which was engraved with a faint pink saw-edged pattern, like a rose quartz. It felt stony and alien—perhaps it was a piece of meteorite from a planet that broke off into my hand. Depending on the light, it sparkled mysteriously of green and pink and transparent white, and I thought it was speaking to me in a new language. Uncle corrected me, telling me that it wasn't a shard of rock, but rock salt harvested from a salt mine. He bought it at a mining village in Catalonia, Spain. Unable to believe that this large rock, as firm and beautiful as a top-quality diamond, was salt, I touched my tongue to its surface. Gradually, saltiness spread in my mouth. It felt as if I'd put at the center of my tongue a grain of sea salt, evaporated by sunlight and obtained after a laborious process; it was that kind of feel-good saltiness. I placed that rock salt on a saucer and put it on the windowsill next to the row of basil, lavender, thyme, rosemary. As Uncle observed, the rock salt was alive. On sunny days it shot out brilliant rays so strong that it blinded you, and when it rained white salt crystals appeared on its surface. Like a small, sensitive animal, the lump of salt seemed to breathe in and out.

Uncle told me a story, a French folk tale, the day he gave me the rock. A long time ago, a princess told the king, "I love you as much as I love salt." Believing it to be an insult, the king banished his daughter from his kingdom. But after a long time, the king realized the value of salt and the depth of his daughter's love for him. I smiled ruefully. Was it because, as a grown woman, it felt pointless to talk about things like this with Uncle? Or was it because I already knew what Uncle was trying to say? I said, So, Uncle, you love me as much as you do salt? in an attempt to make him laugh. But Uncle didn't crack a smile. We were thinking of the same person, our faces rigid. I wished I had pockets full of funny stories, but all I had was a knife.

Uncle had gone to Spain on a two-month-long honeymoon. The day after he gave me the salt, he was admitted to a hospital in Icheon, in Gyeonggi Province. It was his decision, but it had taken a long time for him to reach it. *Sometimes I'm afraid I won't remember her name*, Uncle said, his voice choked. She was once my aunt—it was unbelievable that he sometimes forgot what her name was. Uncle suffered from Korsakoff's syndrome, brought on by alcoholism.

The rock salt isn't getting any smaller.

One morning after a rainy night, I stand by the window, staring at the white crystals on the rock, then call in to take the day off and board the bus to Icheon. Uncle doesn't like it when I visit, but it's my duty as his guardian, as recorded on the hospital forms. Will he feel a little better if I tell him there's no such thing as dead salt, that his beliefs are wrong? As we merge onto Jungbu Highway, the raindrops, mixed with snow pellets, slash across the windshield.

Uncle's the one who told me that salt wasn't just a mineral, but Chef's the one who taught me salt's abilities. Salt retains vegetables' vivid colors when parboiling, removes astringency from salad greens, freezes ice cream, quickly cools boiling water, maintains the freshness of cut flowers, removes stains on clothing, alleviates pain in your neck, is an ingredient in soap. But the most important thing salt can do is cure fish and meat. Without salt, they're the first to go bad. During the salt-curing class, Chef brought out a small, oily herring with a single dorsal fin and a split tail. The herring is washed, its stomach is sliced, its innards removed. It's washed again, then a fistful of salt is sprinkled all over it. When moisture breaks through the surface, the tail of the fish is grabbed and it's shaken in the air once, followed by another liberal sprinkling of salt. No matter how much herring you have, all of this must be done in half a day. Herring is oily, so you can maintain its freshness only if you salt it within two days of capture. Since it has to go through distribution channels, once you have a herring in your hands, the first thing you have to do is quickly salt it. Salt is a blessing as well as an instrument that supposedly wards off evil, used in a ceremony where one places a grain of it on a baby's tongue. If cooks are given a not-so-stellar ingredient, first they salt it, then they figure out what to do with it.

During my stint at Won's Kitchen, I made food for photographic purposes, to accompany interviews with newspapers and magazines. I was often asked which ingredient I most cherished, and every time I would open the wine cooler next to my oversized refrigerator and show them. When we built this kitchen, we'd poured our hearts and souls into the U-shaped marble counter with a hole cut in the middle, through which I could sweep in garbage—but the items I chose with the most deliberation were the fridge and the wine cooler. They were also the most expensive. I kept my salt in that wine cooler.

Grandmother used to say that the taste that came from the hands was the most important element in cooking, that this flowed from the sincerity of the cook, but in my case the most important thing was seasoning the food adequately with salt. Even when salt is only slightly dried out, the important minerals vanish and its taste and scent change. Like wine, it's important to keep it in a place that maintains the perfect level of humidity and temperature. If I had to choose only one seasoning, it would obviously be salt.

But like Chef said, the trend of cooking everything with "a slight sprinkling of salt," in vogue when he started cooking, has passed. If I were to divide the cooks these days into two categories, it would be cooks who don't use salt and cooks who do. Chef is in the latter category. On Nove's special menu, there's sea urchin topped with caviar, and when that dish is served, Chef spreads a thick layer of coarse sea salt on the bottom of a big, half-transparent blue salad bowl, on top of which he places the sea urchin in its shell and a teaspoon. Chef pours the salt into the bowl not purely for decoration but for the diners to dab the sea urchin in—but none of the customers, who now believe that salt is bad for their health, dip the sea urchin in salt. Without that saltiness, eating sea urchin is the same as eating a saltless anchovy. People are attracted to salty foods because of a fundamental biological shield against salt deprivation. The day before the launch party for my cooking school, Chef brought over a jar of transparently bright salt and three loaves of bread baked with only olives, yeast, and salt—maybe Chef wanted to convey to me the significance of this mineral.

I walk into the hospital. In the spring and fall, the place is blanketed with Japanese cornelian cherry, dicentra, maple—more like a resort than a hospital. In reality, Uncle may just need somewhere to rest, not to be cured. Now that I'm alone, Uncle could run with me. Then one of us would be able to walk Paulie, who's the kind of dog that must be walked every day, and I wouldn't have to boil a single egg for breakfast. But I know I'm not ready yet. I still can't forget the terrifying scene I witnessed, of Uncle downing my alcohol-based facial toner. Uncle said his illness was caused by love, but in my eyes it just showed how a woman could ruin a man. Now I know I have to be prepared for a scenario that is the other way around.

I'll wait a little longer. Everyone makes mistakes, and it's not too late to fix things when you realize you've made one. I'll wait until spring, when I'm a little more energized. It's impossible to imagine a world without salt. Everyone needs salt. I'm hurting right now not because we've split up, but because I can't say "I love you" as I did before. If I can't start over with him and go back to the beginning, then I'll make sure I end it exactly as we started it. Holding a thermos of Uncle's favorite spicy seafood soup brimming with tomatoes and basil, I march toward the reception desk.

# CHAPTER 8

THE QUESTION OF why I became a cook is almost unanswerable. It's the same as asking, Why did you fall in love
with that man instead of all these other men? Of course you
can't give a clear reason. This is unexplainable even to the person
you've fallen in love with. I can give an example. Let's say you're
the sun. The sun takes the purest and lightest particles of seawater and lifts them into the air. Salt is left behind because of its
weight and heft, a product of these solar movements. If this is to
be an adequate example, I have to talk about the sun's passion
and motive in making salt. Creating salt is sort of the ultimate
fate for the sun. The importance of salt naturally elevates the
sun's value in the world of gourmandism. Every human act is
only a dream at first. That dream comes to you sometimes like
fate, other times like coincidence, and it can be achieved in unbelievable ways. In my case, it all began with a pheasant.

Twenty years old, I was sitting in my college history class, chin
cradled in hand, daydreaming. I didn't know what I should do
with myself. Twenty years of age is like a pineapple—a crown

tops your body, but instead of being able to merely shave away the peel, a knife is needed to strip off the leaves to get to the inner fruit. You're filled with juice, but the part that can be consumed is wrapped tightly in short, pointy leaves, and you don't yet have seeds or a firm core. My biggest problem was that I couldn't find something I could engage with passionately. While spring was the season in which some people regained their energy, for others it was the season into which they dragged themselves, reeling from the aftershock of winter. All I could get myself to do was look out the window during lectures, bored, facing the clouds slowly drifting in the wind or being embraced by the gentle, light spring breeze.

That day in April, I sat by the window in the lecture hall, the sun just starting to set, captured by a faint hope that maybe being twenty years old wasn't like being a pineapple but more akin to tasting something delicate and fresh and light and textured, like the spring breeze. And I sat there watching as a brightly colored chicken flew into the lecture hall, flapping abruptly into my daydream. It took me a while to realize that it wasn't a chicken but a bird with shorter legs and a longer tail—a pheasant. The lecture hall erupted into chaos.

Still in my seat, clasping my trembling hands tightly, I stared at the strong, slippery-looking pheasant, its bright black eyes shining from near its white beak and red feathers, its dark navy neck speckled with purple, its gold chest, its length of over eighty centimeters. Eventually the professor and a couple of boys managed to capture the bird by the wings, which flapped desperately, and tossed it out the window. The commotion died down, but the professor wasn't able to regain anyone's attention, everyone whispering about the sudden entrance of the pheasant, suggesting that we should have captured it and presented it to the security guard instead of tossing it out the window, or discussing the possibility that it hadn't actually been a male but a female with plain brown feathers, or that it had been a white pheasant that was supposed to be so rare, or that it hadn't been a pheasant at all but a chicken. All these conjectures fluttered lightly around the room along with the bird's feathers, the only proof that a pheasant actually did fly in through the window.

One day when I was little, Grandmother held out something red and round and told me it was an apple. Apple. I remembered the word *apple*. And Grandmother told me to touch it, and asked, What does it feel like? I understood that this thing called an apple was firm and cold and very smooth to the touch. Then Grandmother had me sniff it and take a bite out of it. Each time I had to report what I sensed—it smells nice, it's sour and sweet. I grew up following Grandmother around the orchard, watching pears and apples ripen and fall to the ground, their white, cloudlike blossoms blooming and fading. My sensitivity to and knowledge about flavors is completely a product of Grandmother's unique educational philosophy, taught in the orchard and kitchen. But I don't think I'm as rational as others who are sensitive to taste. I was introduced to the vast, infinite world of sight, sound, touch, taste, and smell by a single apple. Afterward, as I neared puberty, Grandmother taught me how to taste the melding of ingredients and seasonings and evaluate them, introducing me to various tastes and awakening the different parts of my tongue.

After the pheasant's exit, I went back to staring out the window, unconcerned about my classmates' theories. That's when I realized it. I couldn't stop myself from leaping out of my seat. What I needed now wasn't to learn about boring historical events, but the kind of work I could do using my senses of smell, taste, touch, sight, hearing. My eyes had sliced through the pheasant's body as I murmured to myself, You're beautiful, but your firm flesh, if handled by knife and fire, will slide smoothly down my throat. It was the first time I'd talked to a pheasant and the first moment I understood that gourmandism wasn't a simple sense-driven thing, but a clear and rational act. This newfound knowledge of mine whispered to me that I should choose to do something I enjoyed, to live the kind of life I'd be happy in. This awakened in me the impulse to gulp down things I'm strongly attracted to, things I like.

The next day, I dropped out of college and applied to the first Italian cooking school that opened in Korea. I was still twenty years old, but I was a twenty-year-old who had attained something I hadn't had the day before. The light, the kind that only eyes accustomed to the dark could discern—this light captured me.

The crucial question isn't why I became a cook. Going back to the example of the sun: To get to the point where a lot of salt is created, the solar rays have to penetrate deeper, to the core. You can't lose your passionate curiosity toward the man you love, and you have to go to him with your entire being, recklessly and passionately. Right now, what I must question and doubt is: Is this true love? And does he love me? And this is the only question that will never be answered.

# CHAPTER 9

F EBRUARY, THE SHORTEST MONTH of the year as well as
one bereft of holidays, is generally slow for the restaurant
industry. But you can't go home early or work less just because
there are fewer customers. At Nove, February is when we develop a new menu, so it's the month most fraught with emotion
and tension. This is when we devise the new summer menu that
we'll introduce in July.

Like all other things about Nove that have remained constant
in my four years of absence, Chef's practice of coming up with
a new menu twice a year is still the same. Chef sends two cooks
to Italy twice a year, in January and July. It's up to them whether
they want to travel together in one region to visit restaurants or
choose different regions and travel separately. You're supposed
to travel around Italy for fifteen days, eating and drinking and
eating and drinking some more. Nove picks up the tab, and your
sole responsibility is to report on the most memorable dish you
encountered, the dish you want to recommend for the new menu.
Nove creates the new menu based on those reports. It depends on

the person, but once in a while someone brings back the recipe itself, or maybe has learned how to make the dish in the kitchen of that particular restaurant. Most cooks rely on their taste buds to guess which ingredients were used, especially because famous restaurants rarely reveal their recipes. Sure, writing the report was difficult, but it wasn't every day that you got the chance to choose a region to travel through and focus only on eating and drinking and sleeping, for fifteen straight days. Maybe because of opportunities like that, Nove boasts a high retention rate among the staff.

In the six years I worked at Nove, I got to go to Italy five times. I learned how to pair foie gras with baked apple in Tuscany, how to make gelato in Bologna, and assembled pizza margherita in Napoli, working ten days for no pay in the kitchen of the most famous of pizzerias in a city renowned for its pizza—the establishment sold four thousand sheets of pizza margherita a day. There's no better place than Italy to think only of food and to eat three meals a day and drink and sleep. In Italy, if something isn't in my mouth, I'm hungry. And I brought back something else from Italy, not just food.

After all the guests go home, the staff that had gone on the food trip and those who contributed ideas stay behind with Chef, making, eating, judging food late into the night. Anyone who's worked in a kitchen for eleven hours a day would know that food, no matter how delectable, can't always be delicious. But February is a special month. Every day, I get to work by ten in the morning and stay until after midnight, cooking, eating, drinking. If I were to categorize it, the food I eat now isn't the food of solidarity, isn't a peace offering—it's closer to the food of discord that causes my mouth to shut down. Even if Mun-ju didn't voice her concerns about my being too skinny, I do need to gain weight and I don't ever want to be the kind of cook who doesn't eat. As the restaurant gears up to create dishes for the new menu, I start concentrating on eating. Even when the others just taste the new dishes, I finish an entire plate of it, whatever it may be. No matter how sensitive your tongue is, sampling one bite and judging it is akin to seeing someone once and talking about him as if you know everything about him.

Rejection of food: This was the first hurdle I encountered after parting with him. Refusing food is basically a refusal of relationships, and if it gets worse it can turn into a frightening illness, leading to a complete destruction of all human contact. I eat all day until it exhausts me, like Mun-ju used to ten years ago. But the thing that drains me most is not the act of eating but the smells. It isn't the stern and picky Chef that reigns over the small kitchen, but the pervasive smell of food. One is taken prisoner by it.

My problems with Paulie start with smell, too.

When I moved out of Grandmother's house, I didn't realize that I would one day have a dog. The first time I went to his house, I saw a large, flat, shiny brown mound in the middle of the yard, bathed in sunlight. His name is Paulie, he said to me, as if introducing himself. It was the first time I'd met someone who uttered a dog's name so lovingly, making me think that if I were asked why I fell in love with him, I'd say it was because of the way he called, Paulie! Blood rushed to my head, just as it does when you take a sip of sweet, hot liquor, as I wondered how he would call my name if he called his dog like that. I joked that the dog was so big that I thought he was a bear, even though he was hunched on the ground. He let out a loud laugh and said, Hey, Paulie, say hello. Surprisingly, the big dog got up, ambled over, stopped in front of me, and silently and gently pushed his smooth square nose into my knee. Paulie's nudge later became "Are you okay?" in our secret language.

Now it's just Paulie and me, left behind. I didn't believe we would have any problems, though I didn't have all the time in the world to think about this. It would be hard for Paulie to understand that, at times, I don't remember to eat, or that I want to be holed up at home. Just as I forgot that Paulie needs his daily walk and that his teeth-baring bark isn't a threat but a sign of submission. I didn't remember that Paulie couldn't be left at home all day, all alone, since he's such a loyal animal, one who has a hard time whiling away the hours without his owner.

In mid-February, when I start coming home late every night, the house is a complete wreck, Paulie having messed up the books, cushions, clothing. And no matter how close you've grown emotionally, scent is the one thing that humans and dogs disagree about. Paulie and I like entirely opposite scents. Paulie hates the perfume I spritz on, while I can't stand the smell of the urine and feces Paulie deposits on the cushions and carpet. Paulie had been well trained since birth, but after his cherished owner left, he has started going to the bathroom in the house, wherever he wants to. I understand this, of course, since Paulie seems to understand why I sleep so much or why I accidentally pour orange juice instead of water into his bowl. It isn't easy to come home late and clean a house purposely ripped apart by the dog, but it's the smell that's intolerable, the smell of his urine and feces that wafts insistently like rotting eggs from this or that corner. Nothing works. Paulie keeps doing it.

Even if they're of the same breed, dogs are all individuals, like people, and certain dogs have peculiar characteristics. On my way home, I think that I should hurry back so I can take Paulie for a walk, but once I arrive I head toward the bathroom to wash my hair, saturated down to my scalp with the smells of the kitchen, and after the shower all I want to do is fall dead asleep. No matter how much I eat, my body is forever tired. I think spring is coming, I whisper, lying on the sofa and carelessly brushing Paulie's neck with my hand. Paulie shudders suddenly and raises his head, and I smell something. I sniff, flaring my nostrils. What did you do, Paulie? Paulie shakes his head, all the hair on his body fanning out. I remove the hand tangled deep in Paulie's fur and sniff it. It's a smell I know well. That smell is slowly diffusing in the air. I push my hand back into Paulie's coat and Paulie crouches back down again, acquiescing.

The stench of greenish mold blooming on the surface of blue cheese, the whiff from the hunk of aging lamb hanging from the ceiling, the old, stuffy, sour smell wafting from the underarms of a sweat-soaked shirt—amid all these scents, a refreshingly oceanlike scent, as fresh as a winter herring. A lively, visceral scent. The scent of a man—his scent.

Dogs remember us by the footprints we leave on the ground, from the smell of the hand that strokes their backs. This . . . this is the scent we both like.

Paulie shakes his head. I close my eyes. His smell may still be lingering somewhere on this sofa, too. A tiny number of minute particles. Now this scent is evaporating slowly from the house and from Paulie's fur. But it's not just his scent I'm remembering right now. Right, Paulie?

On Tuesdays and Thursdays, the days I had classes at my cooking school, I would go shopping for ingredients at Gyeongdong Market or big warehouses like Costco. We often went together, but if his schedule conflicted I would take the car and go by myself. That day, after I lugged six large plastic bags stuffed with groceries to the door and was changing into indoor slippers, Paulie, who was lying in front of the opaque pocket door dividing the foyer and the living room, got up, padded over, and pushed his snout against my knee, hard. Unlike other times, the push was forceful, almost unpleasantly so, making me take a few steps back.

What's wrong, Paulie?

When a dog acts in an unexpected way, you have to move the way he wants you to move. When I take Paulie for a walk, I can't just tug on the leash if I want to go a particular direction. Instead I have to follow the dog for a moment and gently turn the way I want to go. If I tug on the leash, the dog will obstinately want to continue going the wrong way. I had already learned a lot about dogs from him. Walking backward, I blocked Paulie, who was anxious to go outside, with a gentle and quiet authority. I thought I heard something from behind the pocket door. And it was unusual that Paulie was crouched outside the door like that, when his owner was inside.

Is someone here, Paulie?

As if in slow motion, Paulie slowly pressed his front feet down on mine and lay down. Meaning we should stay out here together.

Do you know who it is, Paulie?

Paulie snuffled and emitted a low moan, almost like a sigh. I had realized when I was trying to teach Paulie words that dogs could express themselves only in a limited way. But the substance of their communication never contained lies.

Move, Paulie, I ordered in a low and firm voice. Paulie's snout stiffened almost noticeably. Paulie was nervous. He kept poking my calf with his nose.

It's okay, Paulie. Move back, Paulie. Do it!

Paulie reluctantly moved behind me, unable to disobey. I approached the pocket door. I placed my palm on the door, and when I put pressure on it the door slid open.

I stood on the other side of the door with Paulie only for a moment, but I must have been imagining all the possibilities of what was there. There's nothing strange in seeing a naked man and woman. It's as natural as having two different tastes mingling in one dish. She was wearing the peach-colored chiffon dress she had worn under a trench coat in the beginning of fall, which made the other students and me exclaim that it was so pretty on her, gathering around her as we touched the fabric.

From the other side of the doorjamb, I thought the chiffon dress was still very beautiful, but that it was too cold to be wearing it in November. Her hands rumpling the hem of the dress raised to her waist, revealing everything, her lips sucked in his scrotum, wrinkly like dried plums, as he perched on the island. His hands were buried in her hair falling over her face as he gently and repeatedly pulled her head toward him and pushed it away.

When I was a girl, Grandmother told me a story. Once upon a time, a man slept for a long time in a tree. It was before there were many people in the world, at a time when dinosaurs flew around. One day the man woke up. Little tufts of clouds floated gently in the sky, and the wind smelled like grass. He realized that it wasn't grass he was smelling, but a fragrant flower. The flower was blooming right under his tree. He shimmied down the tree with his thick, strong legs. A round well of water was pooling in the middle of the wide, big leaf, shaped like a dish. The man stood there, staring down at the water, then bent down and slowly and reverently started drinking it in.

Looking at him, I knew that was what the man in the story must have looked like when he was drinking in the water. He sat her down on the sofa—she was now completely naked—and kneeled and stared at her down there, which must have opened up like a ripe fig, just as if he had woken from a lengthy slumber and was gazing at rainwater collected in a leaf for the first time in his life. His back was to me, but I knew what his eyes looked like. I'd thought those eyes were meant only for me.

He started carefully and rhythmically rubbing her with his finger, massaging her. She spread her legs wider to allow his finger to come in deeper and looked down at his face with an expression like, Look, look at how perfect mine is, then moaned and closed her eyes. Nobody was rushing, nobody was nervous. Meaning that it wasn't the first time they'd had sex. Like people foraging for mushrooms, the two concentrated secretively and carefully in the tense, impatient quiet, pulling and pushing and tensing and tugging at each other like giant, pink, wet, shiny tongues entwined as one. They were completely immersed in eating, as if they were attending a feast not of different kinds of food but of different methods of eating—chewing, sucking, licking. He pulled her bottom, round and blushing like peaches marinated in red wine, onto his lap. Then he pushed against her from behind, gripping her waist with both hands, and I heard him yelling out her name, loudly. As if my eyes were erogenous zones, I shivered too. I wanted to run in and ask, How did it taste?

When you eat peaches marinated in red wine, you have to take an extremely sharp fork and stab it—that's the only way to enjoy it.

# MARCH

*I am offering you the things which you eat,*
*now you must do whatever I demand.*

Tibetan Buddhist Sherpa saying

# CHAPTER 10

WINTER CAME AND WENT like a fish that lost its way. At the same time it was a long, cold, never-ending winter. I'm so glad I was able to survive, I say to myself, quickly feeling better about the world whenever I catch a glimpse of a yellow daffodil pushing through the frozen earth. Spring is a great season for cooks. You can hear things bursting up through the ground, in the mountains and the sea and the fields; it's like opening a can of herring and catching a whiff of the fresh marine smell and the bubbles of salt water that—*pssht!*—shoot up powerfully like an explosion. The best of these sounds is the squirming of squid rising from the depths of the ocean. The captured squid, surprised, twist around and spout dark ink, as if vomiting the wounds they'd been keeping to themselves all winter. They're pleasingly chewy, fresh, and filled with eggs, March and April being peak season, guaranteeing optimal taste and nutrition. March also happens to be the month Nove serves its seasonal squid pasta. After finishing prep, I rest a little, waiting for customers to arrive for lunch, and dip five or six

59

little squid in boiling salt water, fish a piece out, and, instead of pairing it with the traditional Korean condiment of vinegar-spiked red-pepper paste, I dip it in pesto and put it into my mouth. It feels squishy but chewy at the same time, the smell of the sea spreading in my mouth along with the effervescent, fresh taste of basil. It's truly the taste of spring.

Right now I'm making tiramisu. The most representative dessert of Italian cuisine, tiramisu is good at any time of the year, but I happen to think that spring is the best season for it. It's hard to prepare and difficult to keep compared to other cakes, so I don't make it often, but in the spring I send it out to the regulars, on the house. Tiramisu, beloved by eighteenth-century Venetians, means "pull me up" in Italian, as in uplift your mood. Because of the espresso stirred into it, you actually do feel peppier after a bite. In the winter, if you accompany it with a cup of hot coffee garnished with a drop of cognac, the calming effect of the tiramisu is even greater. I make the espresso, and while it cools I put some sugar in a pot and boil it; at the same time I beat eggs, add water, scrape in the seeds of a vanilla bean, and give the whole thing a whirl. It's the first dessert I made with the students at Won's Kitchen, six weeks into the program. I spread cream and mascarpone, drizzle it with espresso, top it with a dusting of cocoa powder, and stick it in the fridge. I'm thinking of taking it out for the afternoon snack after it chills. It's the first snack I've made since coming back to Nove. If a dish is too salty, you fix it with honey, and if it's too sweet, you add some salt. I hope the other cooks will spoon into it gently from the outside corners, slide it into their mouths, and agree: I think K has finally found her rhythm.

The youngest prep cook, Choi, forgot to order salumi and mozzarella, creating problems for dinner service. It's not the end of the world if we don't have salumi, but if we don't have mozzarella, we can't make caprese salads, the most popular appetizer

60

on our menu. Mozzarella demands freshness, so we don't order huge batches of it. To make it worse, today is the day that Mr. Choe—the leader of the most influential group of gourmet eaters, Mido—is scheduled to come for dinner. Manager Park said it would be best not to tell Chef and I'm chosen to go to the closest market this afternoon. I feel a little uncomfortable that the market closest to Nove is actually the Costco in Yangjae-dong, the one I used to frequent with him, but I've already stepped outside into the windy street.

When there is a huge crack in your relationship with some-one, you wonder what others do in similar situations. I realize I'm trying as hard as I can to present myself as the most un-threatening being in the world, like a small animal. I hunch into myself, avoiding going back to the same places I frequented with him. Obviously I don't eat the kind of food we ate or made together. But I don't think I'm going to move to a new house, because I have the kitchen and the large fridge that I'd wanted for so long. People say you can't possibly like your lover every single second of your life. But that's not true. I liked and looked to my lover every single second we were together. And I still can't admit that he's gone. True sorrow is when one person de-sires but the other doesn't. I don't know any better words to de-scribe it, and I can't yet express this feeling through any kind of food. The one thing we know about sorrow is that it's a very personal, individual feeling.

# CHAPTER 11

W HAT DOES A WOMAN DO as she waits for her man? She
may wash her hair, put on makeup, choose the kind of
outfit any woman would be eager to try on, spray on perfume,
and look at herself one last time in the mirror. If she does these
things, it's when she and the man she's waiting for are in love. It's
different when a woman waits for a man she still loves but who
has broken up with her, because the pure joy of it is missing.
Loving someone is like carving words into the back of your
hand. Even if the others can't see the words, they, like glowing
letters, stand out in the eyes of the person who's left you. Right
now, that's enough for me.

I wonder whether I should clean up a little or give Paulie a
bath but instead just end up lying on the sofa. I try to think of
something we did together when he loved me, something that
has to do with me, not with washing Paulie or cleaning up, but
I can't think of anything. Even though I'd once wanted to share
so many things with him, so many things that would make us
happy or excited. I rustle around. By the time he gets here at

two P.M. as promised, I'm deep in slumber. I had been lying in the street just like this when we first met, and when I opened my eyes I saw him looking down at me, his nose almost touching mine. Paulie alerts me to his presence by tugging on the slipper dangling from my foot. I open my eyes. I see him standing just inside the pocket door, looking uncomfortable. *Come here, like before. Come close.* But he doesn't budge. I sit up and smooth my hair.

"How've you been?" His greeting isn't really addressed to me, but not really to Paulie either. He unslings the bag from his shoulders and puts it down on the floor near the pocket door like he's going to leave very soon. Paulie approaches him slowly and licks his outstretched palm. With his other hand, he strokes Paulie's neck. *Paulie's neck is going to smell like you for a while.*

I rise from the sofa. I hadn't wanted him to see me asleep. "Would you like to eat something?"

"No, I already ate."

We'd usually get ready for lunch around two, leisurely, after our midmorning brunch.

"Already?"

"I'll go take a walk with Paulie and be back."

*You haven't been here for more than two minutes!* "Okay, then." I walk toward the kitchen. Paulie glances at me but pads out the door when he hears his whistle. The sound of him whistling. It's been a long time since I heard it. No matter how hard I practice, I can't make the sound. I hear the door closing. What's the best thing to eat at two in the afternoon? I pucker and try to whistle as I open the fridge door. I have potatoes in the fridge, along with zucchini and flour and pasta and an assortment of sauces and frozen fish—flounder, turbot, mackerel—and fresh anchovies and caviar that would be great in a salad. With these I can put together a decent—though not sumptuous—meal. I used to

64

feel I was being given a special privilege every time I opened the fridge.

In the novel *The Edible Woman*, Marian bakes a cake in the shape of a woman for the man who'd tried to make her change but nearly destroyed her. "You look delicious. Very appetizing. And that's what will happen to you; that's what you get for being food," she says. She calls him to her place and displays the cake. When he panics and leaves, she takes a fork and digs in, starting with the feet. It could be that she was only looking to share something with him and feel satisfied. The novel ends with Marian announcing that it's only a cake, as she spears her fork into her cake body, neatly slicing off the head.

Roman women would bake a vulvalike pastry and put it on the table when they were upset with their husbands. A fresco depicting a cake baked in the form of breasts—made from sweet, thick, yellow custard and finished with red cherries perched on top as nipples—adorns a small church in Sicily. When women cook, they're not just doing it for sustenance. An expression of rage and unhappiness and desire and sadness and pleading and pain may lurk in their dishes. Of course, the best kind is food filled with love.

Just as it's important to be happy when you're in a kitchen, the most crucial thing to keep in mind when you cook is the people who are going to eat your food—their tastes, their desires, their likes and dislikes, what will satisfy them, what will move them, what will make them want it again. A cook should understand the people's eating habits, too. People can't change their eating habits easily. They take their habits with them even when they leave home for somewhere far away. When I first started cooking, Chef would often tell us to cook the way our mothers did when we were young. Having had no mother, I changed that word to Grandmother. When I was working at that restaurant in Napoli, the head chef told me that proper

Italian cooking had to give customers the feeling that their grandmother was in the kitchen, and I found myself smiling despite myself. It's not so when I cook for customers or the students I teach, but when I cook for him, I want to make the kind of food that would pique his hunger for me.

Taking lettuce from the fridge, I pause to look out the window, lit brightly by the spring afternoon sun. I look around at everything I have here—a kitchen spacious enough to conduct a cooking class for ten people, an interior and a yard roomy enough for an English setter, and a thirty-one-year-old man, as tall as a palm tree, walking across the yard. They're not things that would come easily to me at this age. I have it all. Even if things have been bad between us, these I can't easily give up. The problem now isn't whether we love each other, but whether we can return to what we used to be. I need to say to him, subtly, suggestively: *Even if we can't return to what we used to be, it can't be completely futile. We can learn something truly valuable as we pick up the broken pieces and float up to the surface. Let's wait until then.* Being inside the house in the spring, with him there, makes me a more positive person, more outgoing and cheerful.

I think I'll make a meatless sandwich of herbs, vegetables, and eggs. There's nothing more fitting for a meal at two P.M. on a Sunday. If it's true that he already had lunch, the filling should be light. I put the cold chicken and the can of smoked salmon back in the fridge. Then I spread a thin layer of butter on the baguette and drizzle it thoroughly with olive oil infused with chopped garlic and thyme. Without the garlic and thyme enlivening the olive oil, the sandwich is boring. I usually add a bit of mayonnaise, but this time I don't, since he's not a fan. Now all I need to do is stack the ingredients. I spread lettuce, spun dry, slices of boiled egg, tomato, cucumber, onion. Usually one baguette is more than enough for the two of us. I cut it into thirds with the bread knife, on a slant, and nestle them in a gauze-covered basket. Even if it's a simple sandwich, you have to choose quality bread, the ingredients have to sing together, and, whether it's thyme or basil, there must be some kind of herb—this is my philosophy for sandwich making.

"Go ahead, try one." I wait for him to take a bite of the sandwich. The person you can eat with is also the person you can have sex with, and the person you can have sex with is the person you can eat with. That's why dates always start with a meal. You get to experience the impulsive expectation and curiosity toward the other person this way first, not in bed. There are many instances when the opposite is true, too. When you eat together, your relationship deepens or takes a step back—it's either one or the other. Eating together, having sex—he and I are used to both, and we also know how to bring it up to the next level.

I eat by myself. I gulp down two pieces of the sandwich. I'm full. I'm satisfied, but not completely. Sharing something and feeling satisfaction from it—now I can't seem to recall how much joy that used to give me.

"Why don't you just take a bite?" Is the sandwich too boring to stimulate his appetite? He doesn't even look at it.

"I told you I don't want to. Why do you keep doing this?"

"Why do you think I keep doing this?"

"It's over, okay, so please stop."

"Over? What's over? You're not being rational right now. Any day now you're going to come back and beg, saying you were wrong."

"That's just not going to happen. And I wish you'd stop going around talking about Se-yeon."

I don't know what he's talking about.

"I mean, you two liked each other back then. Why would you do something like that?"

"I've never said anything about her to anyone."

"Okay. I guess it's Mun-ju, then?"

"Stop it. All you do is worry about Se-yeon, right? Have you bothered to ask me how I've been doing since you got here?"

"If you keep doing that, you really make me out to be the bad guy."

I can't speak.

"I'm sorry. I'm really sorry, but I can't do anything, okay?"

"You can come back. I told you I understand."

"It's not you I want to live with anymore, it's Se-yeon. How many times do I have to keep telling you this?"

"You told me you loved me with that mouth of yours. Don't you remember? Did you forget all of that?"

"Yeah, I did back then. It's all in the past, though."

"Come back to me."

He doesn't say anything.

I lay a hand gently on his arm, near his left elbow. No matter how much you kick off the covers in bed you always have a corner of it covering your stomach—just like that, we'd always been linked together, by one leg, one arm, one hand. "I'll wait."

He pushes my hand away coldly. "It hurts me, too, to think about us ending up like this."

"It's not hurt—you probably feel guilty."

He's silent.

"Isn't that right?"

"I think in the future I should just visit with Paulie in the yard."

I'm shocked.

*If I bake a cake, I think I'll make it in the shape not of my body, but hers, Se-yeon's. Giggling, watching you shiver in disgust, I would pierce the chocolate eyes with a fork and eat them. You would ask, very seriously, How did it taste? How's that? And since you'll be curious about its taste, we can eat the entire cake, from the ankles. How's that?*

He's not standing in front of me anymore. I rush out to the front door. He turns around, pausing as he slides his feet into his shoes. "Look in the mirror," he says to me, his voice softening with pity for me for the first time.

"You, you're about to leave the person you love the most, okay? So think about it just one more time."

"I'm really sick and tired of that kind of talk."

I'm stunned into silence again.

The door closes.

If I turn around, I'd be able to see him one more time, walking across the yard, kindly but sadly hugging Paulie, whispering, See you soon. I'd loved the shadow he casts, as sturdy as that of a grove of trees in the sun. I'm so worked up that all I can do is crumple onto the shoes stacked in the foyer. I'm not sure what this heavy thing is, pressing down on my shoulders—hunger, powerlessness, Paulie. *Okay. Goodbye, just for now. Even if I have everything, you leaving like that—it's like losing everything. Bye. Even when you're with her, you will have to think about me from time to time. I'll continue to piece together my sorrow here, like this.*

# CHAPTER 12

I F THERE HAS TO BE a reason for it, I think Mun-ju and I
became close not only because we're the same age, but also
because I understood her appetite. Mun-ju said she was the eld-
est of five sisters. Pausing after revealing this, she asked me,
Could you turn the lights off?

It was late at night, after her coworkers had left and I'd even
told her about the pheasant I'd encountered when I was twenty
years old, a story I'd never told anyone. I turned out the light in
the kitchen, came back to the table, and extinguished the light
hanging over the table, dangling from the ceiling above Mun-
ju's head. Amid the honks and the intermittent flashes of head-
lights racing by on the eight-lane road outside the restaurant in
the deep of the night, we were floating in a space of zero grav-
ity where we couldn't feel or taste or smell.

My father wanted to raise us very strictly, Mun-ju continued.
Maybe it was because he felt unsettled that he didn't have a
son. He had rules about when we slept, woke up, studied, and
didn't allow us to wear skirts or blouses. My sisters and I had to

grow up like little soldiers. But raising girls like that doesn't turn them into boys, you know? Our relationship got worse after Mom died. My father set strict curfews and even forbade me from hanging out with friends. I think he was the worst with me because I'm the oldest. Once, after a group tutoring session, a boy walked me home, and my father caught us. For a whole month after that, he didn't touch the food I made, like it was dirty. Food was the hardest thing for him to control. Once a week, he'd force me onto the scale and weigh me, saying a fat girl was of no use to anyone. You can't understand how hard that was for me. I wasn't stick skinny, but I wasn't fat either. So I ended up stuffing myself when my father wasn't looking. There was no other way to rebel. I used to keep a whole bag of brown sugar in my purse. When I was sad about something, I ran straight to the fridge. But the odd thing is that I gained weight every day, a lot of weight, but my father didn't say anything about it. And I couldn't stand that either, because it felt like he was ignoring me.

My father would appear in my dreams and say, I'm going to eat you up because that's how much I love you. I got fatter and fatter. At one point I was so fat that I even dreamt that my girth blew the house to pieces. My life's purpose boiled down to this—leave home as soon as possible, which I did when I was seventeen. I think bingeing and starving are really the same. They both have the same purpose—they give you a twisted sense of accomplishment, allowing you to say, I'm the best at bingeing or starving myself. But that really was all I had. I met you at a time in my life when I was thinking that. And your cooking taught me, for the first time, that food wasn't just for stuffing your face, but was supposed to make you feel something. That first day, the roasted duck breast you made, topped with roots of baby spinach, really got me hungry, just by looking at it. That's why I wanted to leave as soon as possible. But then you came after me in the parking lot, asking why I didn't eat it, how could I write an article about it if I'd never even tried it. You really cracked me up. You were so serious! That day, I thought there must be something special about your food. It'd been a long time since I'd eaten something that made me feel as if a weight had been lifted off me. I feel like I spent all of my twenties struggling with something stupid, with eating, with food. I'm really pissed about it, I really am.

I pushed napkins toward Mun-ju, who was crying.

A sated person is different from a hungry one. A hungry one can't be persuaded to do anything, but a full person can be given boundaries and convinced. So after that, I continued to cook for Mun-ju whenever she popped into the restaurant. I just made the portions a little smaller and helped her to eat slowly, and continued to tell her what she shouldn't eat, what she should avoid, what she must eat. Like most intelligent and creative people, she knew what she wanted and how to focus her whole being on what she wanted. She wasn't avoiding food, she was using food to get over her fear of eating. It was unspoken, but that was what we both wanted for her.

A person's appetite is as precious as salt was in the seventeenth century. Trying to go around the salt officials who confiscated and regulated it, women would hide chunks of it in their cleavage and corsets, between their thighs and buttocks. When the officials squeezed those parts of their bodies, the women would burst out crying in pain. The more you try to take it away, the more people try to hide it. What I could do for Mun-ju was not to hurry, but to wait and watch over her patiently as if I were waiting for the last course of the meal to arrive at the table— this was something anyone could do for a friend. If Mun-ju thought this was special, it was special for me, too. I cooked, she ate. I cooked a little, she gradually ate less.

It took about two years for Mun-ju to transform her physique into a pleasantly plump one. Now, even if there's food in front of her, Mun-ju doesn't attack it quickly like a starving person, but has become a woman who knows how to eat a meal leisurely—but with gusto. When she goes on dates, she doesn't go out again with the men who rush into their food as soon as the first course is placed in front of them, and she even makes me laugh, mimicking them. She was able to get rid of a lot, but Mun-ju hasn't been able to rid herself of the fear that she might become fat again—not just yet.

I don't shrink from the fear of gaining weight. For me, the pleasure I get from eating trumps that fear. The taste bud is like a diamond, getting shinier and sparklier the more you polish it. The person with a good appetite is one who wants to live; in the same way, the sense of taste is the first to go when a person loses the will to live. Some people feel alive when they play music, and others feel invigorated when they write or when they shop. These days I'm energized when I eat. I'm ready to eat anywhere, at any time. And there's something in particular I want to eat—an all-consuming desire. When you can't have something, the desire for it becomes more powerful and intense.

I'm staring at the biggest and deepest hole in his face. His tongue moves around, supple, like the tongue of a fish, like a bird's tongue wrapped in soft cartilage, moving carefully, with concentration, like it does when it's eating the tastiest thing—*The. Person. I. Love. Now. Is. Se-yeon*, the dark hole says. Like the bumpy, scaly tongue of a four-legged animal, it's stiff, rough, reddish black. I stare at his red tongue, I want to suck on it one last time. Like a truffle, a tongue renders a woman and a man in a gentler state and is easy to chew on, light and soft. I take a step toward it. *You told me with that mouth that you loved me.* I'm close enough to swallow it whole. *Hold me just one last time*, I beg. *Don't*, he says, and pushes me away forcefully. I'm hot, like boiling oil.

Like a starving person, I crave his tongue. My throat is already lengthening and opening wide, like that of an always-accommodating goose. He pushes my puckered lips away with his hand and backs up. *I'm going to wait for you*, I warn him gently. He licks his lips with his dry tongue, his tongue that looks parched as if all the juices have drained out of it, and says, *That's never going to happen*. At one point it was a familiar and beautiful tongue, filled with admiration and praise for my body as it understood and explored me. I grab and swallow the whole thing down. His tongue resists in my mouth, like a flopping fresh fish. I grip my mouth closed to stop it from escaping. My teeth grab it swiftly and mash it. My muscular tongue wets it with flowing saliva, works it, flips it, moves it deep into my throat. My tongue bends back to push it in deeper, to shove it down completely. Nothing, not one piece, not one drop, escapes from my mouth. It slides perfectly into my stomach. All the nerves in my body vibrate faintly like the end of a needle, and finally I heave a breath out. My tongue, remembering the dish I've just tasted, licks my lips.

The food I eat in my imagination is more powerful and particular than what I consume in reality, just as a dream feels very real seconds after you awake from it, just as a person thinking about killing someone first tries it out in his dreams. You go over it again and again in the imaginary world because you're deprived of whatever it is you want, because there's something in you that misses it—an unfinished piece of art. Human beings sprint toward pleasure. Unfortunately they feel pain, a joining of sensations, more easily than pleasure.

# CHAPTER 13

I'M LEFT BEHIND with the silent old dog, just the two of us.
When a dog realizes his noises are no longer being understood as language he stops barking and whining. Language exists between people and also between a person and a dog.
Paulie's the one who taught me that, and his silence now signifies my own. If I thought I would return to Nove after we split
up, I might not have taken Paulie. It's not that I'm not fond of
him, but I would have known I wouldn't be able to take care of
a dog. Paulie no longer approaches me happily or wags his tail
or whimpers. But he hasn't turned aggressive or mean like dogs
left to fend for themselves. He seems confused about the
changes in his life and needs time to accept them. As a dog
grows old, the smallest change in his routine becomes the
source of great confusion. I gently stroke Paulie's neck as he lies
on the floor like a pile of dirty brown rags. Nervousness and
unease unite us now. It's invisible but we feel the same thing.
For the first time in a very long while, Paulie's rough tongue
licks my palm and his slightly averted black eyes study my face

as if to say, I haven't forgotten all of this yet. As if he under-
stands whatever I have to say. But it will be almost impossible to
get Paulie to comprehend that he's gone. For Paulie this concept
is more difficult than understanding when he's allowed to jump
up and when he isn't.

It'll be okay, Paulie.

Paulie lets out a moan, the sound being dragged up from the
bottom of his stomach. I hug him and he glues himself to my
body. If only someone were next to me, someone who can understand everything I say. I'm glad I'm not alone but somehow I
get the feeling that I will be left by myself soon.

We fall into a comfortable rhythm. When I come home from
work I take Paulie out for a walk no matter how tired I am. We
usually head to the playing field at the neighborhood elemen-
tary school. I didn't know that so many people exercised in the
field that late, approaching midnight. Before, we walked Paulie in
the afternoon and almost never went anywhere at night. The eve-
nings dashed by as we cooked and ate and listened to music and
played fetch with Paulie in the yard and drank tea. On one of
those nights, I watched him play with Paulie in the yard as I
cradled a cup of tea and realized that this evening enveloping
me was the pinnacle of my life, a solid and brilliant crystal.
Everything was in its place and I had everything I had ever
wanted and we were still so young. One final sentence was left
in the story: They lived happily ever after. His whistle still rings
clearly in my ears and I still see Paulie energetically leaping after
the ball. And all I have left from that evening is the old dog and
the ball nestled in my palm.

Was our love real? I gaze at the ball in my hand. Paulie barks.
I wind up and throw it and Paulie jumps up into the sky, showing off, and catches it in his mouth. Then, his head raised high
with pride, he drops the ball at my feet. I throw it again, far.
His brown hair flying, Paulie darts after it. When Paulie runs

he is more beautiful and more alive than when he pads along slowly, reluctantly. Paulie doesn't tire of chasing after the ball. I want to go home. I want to know if our love was real.

I mime throwing the ball. Paulie leaps up and wags his tail and rubs against my legs and sends me signals—Throw it, throw the ball already. *I'm tired. Let's go home, Paulie!* Paulie focuses intently on my hand that holds the ball. He's more excited now than he had been during the actual game of fetch. I raise the ball high above my head and start running backward. Paulie springs up into the air ever more powerfully, over and over again. Not being allowed to touch the ball works him into a frenzy. Is the game of fetch not about sharing the ball but about heightening pleasure by drawing out the anticipation? I may have just discovered something new. I slowly squeeze the ball, solid and responsive to the touch.

When I first started offering cooking classes, Mun-ju guaranteed she would take care of everything, especially attracting students. Since she worked in publishing from the moment she entered college, she was the one in our group with the heftiest address book. But it turned out there was a steady demand of women who wanted to learn how to cook. Not as a hobby, but to satisfy a growing interest in eating better. These days, being a good cook is just as admirable as speaking a foreign language or playing an instrument. And after a while the number of male students multiplied, probably because women are attracted to men who know how to cook. Although it was sweet to see couples signing up for classes together, I preferred living with someone who didn't know how to make a thing. I need to be with someone who waits for my food, who eats my creations.

One day Mun-ju brought a new student to class, a woman wearing a minidress in a large floral print, her hair tied with a retro silk scarf and holding a brown tote, so tall she stood out wherever she went. Every part of her appeared to be made with care. Her name was Lee Se-yeon. Mun-ju introduced us, explaining that she had met the former model while working for the now-defunct *Fashioniste*. I remembered seeing her when I worked at Nove. She was a VIP and sometimes rented out the place for a gathering or to throw a party. At first she came once a week to the Bread and Cooking class, and after about a month she registered for Italian Cooking, appearing in my kitchen twice a week. She walked into our house looking like a well-dressed mannequin in a show window, legs as long as a flamingo's. Though she had retired from modeling she remained attuned to trends and enjoyed standing out in a crowd. She was the kind of woman who couldn't stand not to be noticed. She was slender, as if she was terrified of eating and only lapped up the juices seeping out of fruit. It was hard to believe that someone like her wanted to learn how to cook. Deceptively, she ate more than her physique suggested and enjoyed it. When I discovered that she made a beeline for the kitchen when entering her house like the rest of us, my trepidation melted away. She appeared even more luminous—raindrops thrown into the spotlight. If I were a man I would want to take her to an isolated island and have her to myself. And she would have to spend the rest of her life there.

While we waited for the food to finish cooking in the oven, we usually gathered to drink tea or make a snack. If he was upstairs in his office, he came into the kitchen to grab a bite. The more that time passes, the more I think of the first time she saw him: She raised her eyebrows and widened her eyes just for a moment, then she slightly turned her face away, pretending to look elsewhere. Then she glanced back at him gently and smiled, her eyes open wide. It was an audacious and gorgeous smile. That brief second lingered for a long time; the air stopped moving. Her smile was so frank and confident that I couldn't help but let out a laugh. He looked at me while she looked at him and I at her. She passed by and I smelled marjoram. A hint of marjoram remained in my kitchen the next day. It was early last fall.

I feel relief when I touch something firm. I grip the ball. If nobody wants what you have you might feel it's nothing much. *So the only thing left to do is to bring the ball back, Paulie. You feel it too, right? Sorrow barreling in from the left and rage rushing in from the right.* I wind up and toss the ball as hard as I can. Paulie leaps into the night sky. Even though he's tame, he's an animal with knifelike weapons adorning his mouth—like humans.

# CHAPTER 14

Y OU'RE IN CHARGE of the private party tonight."
I'm shocked into silence.

Chef stares at me, his hands in his pockets. It's his way of putting his trust in me, scrutinizing my creativity and skills. This is the first time since I restarted at Nove. There must be a VIP coming in today. My excitement billows, like the first time I held a knife in Grandmother's kitchen.

"What are the mains?"

"You decide."

I'm surprised.

"The person who reserved wanted you to put together a menu."

This is rare. If customers are this familiar with the restaurant, they reserve through the desired cook.

"Who is it?"

"The bass is fresh and the duck is nice, so do what you want."

I don't say a thing.

"You're a cook."

"If you don't tell me who it is, I'm not doing it."

I hear the tap-tap-tap of rain. For a gloomy day like this, duck is better than sea bass, and a hearty cut of steak served after thick, steamy pumpkin soup is best. My mind is already whirring but I don't back off. I have to know who it is. Chef and I stand facing each other, hands in our pockets. We keep our hands deep in our pockets, worried that they smell. A knife is an extension of our fingers, so unless it's a special occasion our hands are safer inside a pocket.

"It's Lee Se-yeon."

I'm stunned.

Whenever Se-yeon rented out the restaurant to throw a party, I thought she must be a gourmet. Anyone who easily brings people together is surely a gourmet. But she isn't a born gourmet. A natural gourmet appreciates beauty but doesn't steal something that belongs to someone else. It's not surprising that she's coming to Nove for a meal. But who is she coming with?

I can't help but ask.

"What does that have to do with you in the kitchen?"

"If I'm to make the food it has to do with me."

"With Han Seok-ju. They're going to have dinner with their parents." Chef says it quickly as if it's an annoyance, his brow furrowing.

Han Seok-ju. I almost ask, Who is that? "So . . ."

"Yeah, she asked that you take care of their table."

I don't say anything.

On rainy days I want to eat a bowl of something warm, not too much and not too little, and lie in my bed. If he is next to me, I want us to slide into making love, feeling each other's wet tentacles like snails in the rain. What I don't want is to go into the kitchen to be smothered by smells. I really don't want to cook for the woman my man fell in love with. If I pushed my face into the rain nobody would hear my laughter. Not even Chef, who stares into my eyes, reading me like a book. It feels like blood is pooled at my temples, stretched taut.

"I'm going home," I announce.

"Get into the kitchen."

"Let me go home."

"Hurry up and make the menu."

"Chef!" I glare at him as if he's Seok-ju.

*Are you going to back down?* He glares back. *Don't be stupid.*

"What they want is the best Italian food they can get. That's why they're coming here. And they want you to cook it. Isn't that acknowledgment that you're the best cook? If I were you, I would want to go straight into the kitchen."

"I'm not that crazy to think that."

"I'll make you a cup of tea."

"Am I being made a fool?"

"It's simple. Just cook."

"I don't do it for just anyone."

"They're customers."

"They're not just customers to me, Chef."

"Yeah, they're very special customers."

I'm quiet.

"Make something special." Chef points his chin at the rain pattering on the window. "Or make salad with that," he says, awkwardly, like he's trying to make a joke. A long time ago, with the same expression, he told me about a gourmet Chinese emperor who held a contest to select his personal chef. Chefs from around the country presented various delicacies but couldn't excite the rarefied taste of the emperor, whose eyes had been opened to great food at a young age. The emperor was disappointed. But one chef made a raindrop salad and a raindrop omelet, followed by a raindrop roast, and finished with raindrop ice cream. The emperor ate everything happily, exclaiming at its deliciousness, and gave unprecedented praise. Then, to ensure that nobody else would ever eat such a special meal, he executed the chef.

"Go ahead, go into the kitchen. You'll find what you want there."

What I want. What is that?

"I might fail." I look out the window to the road, slippery like the back of a whale, the cars gliding by and the rain slashing across the inky sky. I want to go somewhere far. Would bass be good, or duck? I want to disappear without a trace. Se-yeon likes bass and Seok-ju likes duck. Cooking is the last thing I want to do. Even the most delectable food vanishes in an instant. Did we really love each other? What can I be certain about? If I didn't know how to cook, what would I have left? The sound of rain awakens my ears, hundreds of small fists pounding on the windows.

There isn't much time before they are to arrive. It's just as important to prepare food on time as it is to make tasty dishes. And to bring out the completed dish in a relaxed and leisurely way, without appearing rushed. Food disappears in the blink of an eye but taste lasts for a long time, the taste that explodes on the roof of your mouth and the tip of your tongue. The memory of that taste bobs to the surface when you least expect it. When a certain taste enthralls you, there comes a time when it's difficult to free yourself from it.

As if drawing a gun, I carefully take my hand out of my pocket and lift it up. The hand that moves coldly and quickly when dealing with fish, hot and passionately with meat, infinitely gentle and secretive when touching him. I have this hand even if her body is beautifully perfect.

I brush the blade of the knife with the tip of my fingers. The blade is still sharp, alive. You need a sharp knife to cut evenly, to slice without harming an ingredient's cell structure. A dull knife pierces the ripe cells of meat or fish, lessening its taste. I'm satisfied with the blade. I grab the duck. After turkey it's the second-largest bird, with a grand and intricate taste. I will stuff it with chestnuts and brush its surface with olive oil and herbs and roast it in the oven. With the handle of my knife I gently tap the duck's head, lying limp. It's my fate to love and cook. Loving and cooking are different but also the same. I raise my knife high and bring it down precisely on the duck's legs, spread neatly across the chopping block.

*Okay, come on in. I'll make you such good food that you'll want to kill me.*

# APRIL

*Warm food, pie, and cake were presented on forty plates, along with a variety of poultry. But a poor goose laid an egg on the table, out of fear.*

—Count Khevenhueller, 1756

# CHAPTER 15

U NCLE TREATED WOMEN with various problems. One
woman was so sensitive to smell that she couldn't eat a
thing. Another woman was fine when she spoke, but when she
opened her mouth to chew, pain shot up her neck and shoulders.
One woman had a fit when she heard the word *carrot,* and yet
another woman ate only clementines. Uncle talked about them
as if they were suffering from different diseases but I thought
they shared the same illness. They had never eaten a good meal
or they didn't know how food tasted or they didn't know what
to eat and how to eat it. But it wasn't that simple to Uncle. Uncle's job was to cure these women, and of all his patients, he fell
in love with the one who ate only clementines.

Uncle likened the consciousness of humans, of which he said
six sevenths was submerged below the surface, to stew. Thick,
made with stock, simmered for hours with cubes of beef and
carrots and cabbage and potato. A copper stew pot has a thick
bottom and a long, sturdy handle, and any ingredient you put in
it will instantly lose shape and melt. When steam starts to hang

above the pot and vapor spreads through the air, the fronts of your eyes get cloudy. Nobody knows if I'm crying or smiling as I'm making stew, and only the cook knows if the stew is made of vegetables or a pheasant's head or a pig's liver or a dirty sock.

My first impression of Uncle's wife was that—how do I say this—she looked like a young calf. Pale, pinkish skin; skinny, large, black shining eyes, frozen by fear. And over her mouth she wore a mask as if to say, I'm not ever going to eat. But she also held a fork and knife in each hand at the table, as if she were going to eat somehow. She was your typical neurotic. Apparently a big sharp fork with one bent tine weighed on the subconscious of Mrs. N, Freud's patient, which was why she couldn't eat and was always hungry. When she was a young girl, her father had punished her if she balked at eating a piece of meat that had grown stone cold, its fat congealed. Uncle thought there must be something like a sharp fork with a bent tine looming over his wife, too, but he was unable to discover what it was. Uncle took it slow, as if he were cooking a rice dish. Back then Uncle was radiant— I thought it was the look of a man in love. But his wife showed me that so many women don't want to eat and that food could be the cause of the most excruciating pain. This refusal to eat is not the same as drinking around the white film that forms atop hot cocoa or milk or cooled porridge. Not eating something you dislike doesn't bring about pain that is evocative of death.

Eating is an absolute, repetitive activity. The same as love. Once you start you can't stop. So if you can't eat when you're hungry, it's worse than being stricken with the gravest illness. Uncle's wife, who possessed a flickering appetite, committed suicide in the most dramatic way—she slathered oil all over her naked body and hanged herself. It may have been a rebellion against things she couldn't eat, or perhaps it was a painful ritual of self-sacrifice. Was it resignation or a holy ritual? If it was her intention to be remembered by the strongest last image, she got her wish. Even now I sometimes think of her dangling from the ceiling, her emaciated body glistening with oil.

Uncle dreamt about her often after her death, and he said that in his dreams he's always examining her teeth. Every time I imagined Uncle stretching his neck out to look deep down her throat, I felt a pain that might split my chest in two. I don't know if the pain came from sadness or an instinctual anxiety. I started to resent his wife. Death requires more love from the one left behind. I hoped Uncle would meet another woman, someone who knew without a doubt what she wanted to eat. But Uncle didn't fall for anyone else and instead quickly started to depend on alcohol. It was the most definite and easy way to forget, but it was also the beginning of a disease that was nearly impossible to cure.

His doctor raised with me the issue of my noncommittal behavior toward Uncle—it wasn't helpful to ignore and protect Uncle as he continued to drink, as it downplayed the reality that alcoholism is a real disease and may have been hindering Uncle's recovery. And that it's hard to continue drinking without someone condoning it. He told me all of this in a reproachful tone, as if he had actually peeked into my thermos. That's probably why he called me to the hospital today. I wonder if I need to defend Uncle or myself.

Uncle stayed with us for six months before he went into the hospital. One day, Seok-ju came back from walking Paulie with Uncle and said, worriedly, that he kept falling down. The cabbage I was holding dropped on the floor. Thump. The dense sound rippled in the air, like a bad smell acting as a warning. Falling over is one of the first symptoms of Korsakoff's syndrome. I don't think we should leave him by himself, he said, approaching me and gently pulling my shoulders toward him. Six months, though neither long nor short, was enough for Uncle to acknowledge that the disease had progressed beyond his control, leading to his decision to admit himself to the hospital. Shedding his doctor's coat, Uncle wobbled into the hospital where he'd worked.

You can say that because you've never seen him fall down again and again, I want to tell the doctor. Right now I'm the only person here for Uncle. What else would I be able to do for him, except to bring him this small thermos? Is that what I'm supposed to say? I don't say anything in the end. Because I don't want to appear oblivious. Because Uncle is the only person who knows that the taste of love encompasses the wilted, the overly ripened, the rotten, and the bitter.

Uncle is sitting on a bench, a thin camel cardigan draped around his shoulders over his hospital garb. He sits there leisurely, not waiting for me but as if he's relaxing after a light meal. He glances back at me, his eyes squinting in the sun. Right now there's nothing for us to do but smile at each other. He looks too thin but it may be better to pretend not to notice. Uncle must also be thinking things about me but not asking.

"So I was thinking, Uncle."

"Hm?"

"I'm glad it's spring."

"Yeah, it's already spring. But even in April, it's still cold in the shade. Here, it's hard to tell if the seasons are changing."

"Then let's leave."

"Why, all of a sudden?"

"You're not home here."

"This can be as good a place as home."

"It'd be nice if you came and looked after Paulie and other things."

"Things are still hard for you, I guess?"

I don't say anything.

"I'm still more comfortable here."

"What are you afraid of, Uncle?"

He's quiet.

According to his doctor, the most important thing for Uncle right now is to decide when to end treatment. During his stay, he repeatedly cycled through drinking and quitting—which only made him realize that nothing had changed—followed by guilt and dejection. His doctor says the mere idea of ending the treatment causes Uncle enormous anxiety.

"Have faith, Uncle."

"Faith in what?"

"Faith that you won't drink again."

"You know I can't ever have that."

I don't argue.

The doctor, once Uncle's colleague, tried to reassure me by saying that treating an alcoholic was a very worthy job. I nodded, but I don't know how worthy it really is. Never having a drink is difficult to put into practice. An alcoholic is completely cured not when he doesn't drink a drop of alcohol, but when he's able to control himself and drink a moderate amount. Uncle knows this. Just as he can't completely stay away from alcohol, he can't erase memories of his late wife. Should Uncle bury those feelings deep down, or try to forget her? If Uncle can't regulate his drinking, it's his choice, not the result of a lack of willpower. So it's not up to the doctor or me to decide when to terminate treatment. All we can do is watch over him. Perhaps Uncle needs time to realize that alcohol isn't necessary in his life and that he can survive without drinking. As his family, I have to decide whether I will participate in his treatment.

"What do you want me to do, Uncle?"

"If I think I need help, I'll request it from you."

"Request is a strange word, Uncle."

"Is it? Then I'll ask you for help." Uncle's smile is wide, showing all of his teeth.

There are times when you should listen to the doctor. The

doctor told me that the patient's family has to determine when to be active in the treatment and when to step back. If you become involved too quickly, it can trigger avoidance or anger. This is enough for today. I get up from the bench and dust off the back of my pants.

It's difficult for an alcoholic to stop after the first glass. Drinking becomes a defense mechanism, and when someone tries to stop him, he gets more aggressive, destroying not only himself but also his loved ones. An alcoholic like Uncle has to understand two things: that he can't drink less or quit in one fell swoop, and that he can't ever give up trying. Alcoholics believe that they can limit themselves and trust that they have the willpower to quit. Neither is true. But I'm confused. Am I talking about Uncle or about myself?

# CHAPTER 16

"I HATE ONIONS." Mun-ju frowns, glancing at the chopping board.

I am carefully slicing onions into rings, taking care not to ruin their shape. I smile. Grandmother valued the onion, just after garlic and the potato. On Grandmother's death anniversary, the first food I make to honor her memory is onion pancakes filled with meat. "What's so bad about them?"

"Everything. Their shiny hardness and their smell and their white color. They look exactly like testicles." Mun-ju never met Grandmother but came over to cook with me at every death anniversary and to drink the ceremonial wine to honor Grandmother's spirit. She is trimming mushrooms to be skewered.

"So you don't like garlic, either?"

"Come on, stop laughing."

"It's funny. You like garlic but not onions."

"So? Onions are onions and garlic is garlic."

"They're in the same family, though."

"Plus I had a dream about onions last night."

97

I should have made the onion pancakes before Mun-ju got here. I quickly finish slicing the onions and rinse them in cold water. Mun-ju's dreams are quite structured and colorful—of course, the person who has the dream and the person who analyzes it see the same thing differently, and if I had her dreams I wouldn't call them colorful. I've dreamt about tomatoes several times, baring a segment of my unstable unconsciousness as if I were a holey block of Emmentaler.

"What was the dream?" I ask.

"I was lying in bed and the door opens and a man with a tray walks in, holding the onion dish I hate the most. He rubs it all over my face and tries to shove it into my mouth. I tried so hard not to open my mouth that when I woke up my jaws were sore."

Mun-ju looks calm. Last time, she'd dreamt she was so thirsty that she hacked at a hard palm and cracked it open, getting drenched when all the juices dribbled out. A more visceral dream was the one in which dirt-caked carrots pushed through her body, one by one. Mun-ju's dreams are filled with grinding teeth and swallowing and being eaten up and bitten and chewed, violent and aggressive like an imaginary world created by a child. I wonder what Uncle would say if I were to tell him about Mun-ju's dreams. *People you need aren't there for you.* Maybe Mun-ju wouldn't want to relate those stories even if Uncle were here. If only the dreamer could accurately translate the dream. It's a positive sign that Mun-ju no longer rinses out her mouth after eating or dreaming.

Mun-ju now enjoys food, but she still has a hard time with sex even though the fundamental sexual instinct is oral. I find it interesting when sexual, but not oral, repression exists. Is it because we become aware that we have a tongue before understanding we have a penis, a mouth before a vulva? The organs located in the lower regions, the penis and the anus, feel pleasure by contracting and retaining, which relates to control and obsession, but the mouth is associated with immediate pleasure: sucking, licking, biting. You can try to control your mouth through eating. And although everything involved with eating—swallowing, chewing, digesting, and going to the bathroom—can be orgasmic, achieving an orgasm requires a will. So the urge to maintain control over yourself compels you to control your food intake, then represses your sexual urges. We neither know how to cure it nor do we have the courage to do so. Liking or disliking something is a conceptual problem, not a real one. It's the same even for dogs.

"Grandmother once had a dream about onions," I remember.

"What was it about?"

"She found a trunk, and she opened it to find shiny gold onions. It wasn't money or gold, but Grandmother thought it was a good omen. Onions shimmering like gold—a whole trunk's worth at that! Grandmother thought she saw something that doesn't exist in this world, like the ancient Egyptians used to."

"Egyptians?"

"If you look at an onion sliced in half, you see concentric circles. Egyptians thought this mirrored the concentric circles of the heavens and believed that onions and garlic had powerful healing properties. So they packed onions inside mummies, and when a loved one died, they placed them in their eye sockets."

"That's kind of disgusting."

"Well, I know you don't like onions, but try to look beyond that."

"Was your grandmother a happy person?"

"I think so. At least before her son and daughter-in-law died in the accident."

"I think I would be different if I had a grandmother."

"What do you mean?"

"I don't know, maybe I wouldn't have grown up hating the kitchen." Mun-ju smiles.

That might be true. Mun-ju's mother died before Mun-ju was old enough to learn how to cook by her side. You don't enjoy cooking if you think of it as a duty. Mun-ju couldn't understand that the kitchen is a warm, cozy place—Grandmother used to say that being in the kitchen is like sitting close to someone in front of the fireplace on a winter night. Even if I'm preparing food for a death anniversary, I'm not making the dishes for a dead person: It's as if Grandmother is scheduled to come in five minutes, holding dried lavender in one hand and a basket of steamed potatoes in the other. Filled with excitement and expectation, I season fernbrake and boil chicken and fry beef and onion pancakes. The first time I cooked a full-course meal was on the date of Grandmother's death, the year after she died.

"If I picked up that trunk, I wonder what would have been inside?" wonders Mun-ju, still thinking about onions.

"I don't know. What would you want to be inside?"

"Hm, I'm not sure."

"Something you like, I'll bet."

"So something like water?"

What am I supposed to say to that? You can't go back after a potato has cooked through or an egg has been broken. *Just forgive your father, Mun-ju.* Otherwise Mun-ju might continue torturing herself with these dreams. Dreams where nobody can help her.

"What would be in it if it were you?" Mun-ju asks.

"In the trunk?"

"Yeah."

"I don't know . . ."

I don't think it's appropriate to say tomatoes, but I can't

think of anything else. Once when we were young, Uncle said, Want to see something interesting? and pulled down his pajama bottoms. There's a flesh-colored pinky dangling between Uncle's legs, I thought, and immediately fainted. I also fainted after I first slept with Seok-ju, as if I were a woman living in the nineteenth century who'd bitten into a tomato for the first time. The tomato was an emblem of fear and terror for me: With its thick, sticky innards and densely embedded black seeds, it was as if I were touching something forbidden. My hidden sexual orality slowly drifted downward, like rain trickling down a tree branch. Seok-ju licked it and smelled it and touched it and wet it like it was a small fruit that would burst and lose its juices if he didn't take care of it, and he waited for it to ripen and open up like a fig. That's how I was able to get over the tomato, although it took almost a year.

I remember making a tomato dressing to go with a seafood salad at one of my cooking classes. I told my students that it's best to find a just-picked, fresh, juicy tomato, although it's hard to find one in the city. One student joked, Isn't that what men want in a woman? Now my face turns red for no reason, like it did then.

"Who said that?" asks Mun-ju.

"I don't remember."

"Se-yeon?"

I don't say anything.

"God, that's so her."

"Yeah, Se-yeon is red and pretty like a tomato."

"You're ridiculous. Just watch, you're going to dream about a tomato tonight." Mun-ju throws a mushroom at me.

"Can you look after Paulie for three days?"

"Are you going somewhere?"

"Yeah, Singapore."

"Oh, it's already April."

"I don't think I can put him in a kennel this time. He's really on edge."

"Ask Seok-ju. Then Paulie will get better quickly, too."

"You know she doesn't like him."

"It's three days! She can't watch him for three days, the dog of the man she can't live without?"

"You'll do it, right?"

Mun-ju is quiet.

The most potent of canine abilities is detecting and isolating a preferred scent from a whole tangle of smells. In the beginning of spring, Paulie stopped smelling like Seok-ju. Even when Paulie's next to me, his ears are pressed back against his head and his tail lists limply to the side. It's the position he assumes when he's about to defend himself. It must be hard for Paulie that the person he needs is no longer around. It's gotten harder and harder to leave Paulie at home by himself. And now I'll be gone for three whole days. After Seok-ju, I cherish Uncle and Mun-ju the most, and so does Paulie.

"It's hard. It feels like it's getting harder and harder," sighs Mun-ju.

"What is?"

"Just . . . everything. Life."

I'm sure it's not everything. There were moments when it wasn't hard. I had many moments when I was happy.

"It's okay, Mun-ju."

"What is?"

"Just . . . everything."

"That's lame."

I want to tell her that onions aren't always bad. That it's better to dream about onions than not to dream at all. Because dreaming must be proof that you're thinking nonstop about the thing you desire. But why does desire come hand in hand with repression?

At one side of the table I put a salad of lettuce, three kinds of herbs, thinly sliced onions and cucumber, and lightly fried tofu with an Asian-inspired dressing. In April, and when you feel tired and lethargic, salad is the perfect choice. Not too stimulating, yet it will put a bounce in your step.

Mun-ju falls asleep. I close the front door and windows, which I'd left open a crack, and turn off the lights. There might be a sign that Grandmother came for a visit. I take a blanket and cover Mun-ju with it. I gently take Mun-ju's hand, poking out from under the blanket, for a little bit. When you're falling asleep, your senses slowly drift to sleep, too. The first one to go is taste, then sight, then smell, then your sense of hearing gradually falls asleep, too. Touch is the last sense to be lulled to sleep. Always alert until the very end, to warn us of any impending danger. In sleep, Mun-ju's cheeks glow like rubies in the dark. Everyone shines like that, sensually, as they fall asleep. The sex you have before sleeping is the most profound and intimate. But when you're finally asleep, all senses become isolated. What would be in my trunk other than onions or tomatoes or water?

# CHAPTER 17

I N APRIL SINGAPORE, also known as "The Earth's Kitchen"
or "The World Capital of Food," hosts the World Gourmet
Summit. This year seventy events will be held for three weeks at
fourteen restaurants and seven first-class hotels downtown, including the Conrad Hotel near City Hall. The summit is famous
for its renowned chefs, who come from all over the world to cook
and satisfy appetites and teach master classes. You can taste the
works of Michelin-starred chefs and converse with them without flying all the way to Europe. Anyone who works at Nove for
at least six months can attend for educational purposes.

This year Chef is leaving Manager Park in charge of the
restaurant and going to the summit with the most junior cooks,
Choi and Kim. It's rare for Chef to accompany them, and it's
even more surprising that he suggests that I attend a wine
workshop. There is always more to learn, Chef says. I know this,
but hearing it pains my heart. His voice reveals that he knows
I'm wavering in the kitchen between chicken and duck, eggplant and onion. Or you can just take some time to rest, Chef

says. I don't recognize this version of Chef—I'm looking at someone who's usually curt but who has suddenly turned very sweet. A man who is stern and standoffish should continue to be like that until the day he dies. It wouldn't be as sad. *I'm not saying you should go to the summit and just rest. You have to eat something different for every meal.* I nod. Chef might be more worried about my eroding sense of taste than about my well-being. When a cook starts to lose his sense of taste, the best way to cure it is to leave the kitchen and eat food prepared by other cooks. Just as the best way to treat someone with an eating disorder is to bring him into the kitchen and have him make something. Three days. It's also a chance to test myself, to see if I can go without thinking about Seok-ju. As we board the plane I mumble, At least it's not an entire week.

We're staying at the Metropol, which is a seven-minute walk across the bridge from City Hall, where the five-star hotels are clustered and where most of the events will be taking place. Chef and Kim are sharing one room and Choi and I will share the other. As soon as we get to the hotel we disperse according to each person's schedule of events. Singapore in April is busy and humid and congested. I change into a cotton skirt, a white T-shirt with sleeves I can roll up, and light sneakers. If Seok-ju were here he would tease, All white again? Even when I wear sky blue it has white polka dots on it; if I wear a striped T-shirt, the stripes are white. You always have to wear white, like a birthmark! he'd say, smiling as if he'd discovered something amazing. I wear white in the kitchen, to feel at home. I smooth the front of my clothes and decide to go eat laksa.

Singapore bursts at the seams with gourmets from all around the world. To determine who is a gourmet and who is not is as uncertain a dilemma as figuring out where a duck's head starts and its body ends. It's not important whether someone is a gourmet. Everyone wants to eat and knows that food is crucial to live. But everyone has his own special reaction toward food. One person can become so excited about a certain dish that his eyes sparkle and his muscles harden, while someone else shovels in the same dish without paying any thought to what he's eating. A gourmet appreciates beauty. Gourmets eat slowly and thoughtfully experience taste—they don't rush through a meal and leave the table as soon as they're done. People who are not gourmets don't see cooking as art. Gourmandism is an interest in everything that can be eaten, and this deep affection for food birthed the art of cooking. Other animals have limited tastes, some eating only plants and others subsisting solely on meat, but humans are omnivores. They can eat everything. Love for delicious food is the first emotion gourmets feel. Sometimes that love can't be thwarted, not by anything.

Foie gras is the most popular gourmet food, but it isn't always easy to come by. In the 1970s, America banned the import of foie gras because of certain illness-causing bacteria. But even this international barrier couldn't stop Jean-Louis Paladin, the world-class chef who was at the helm of the famed Napa restaurant in Las Vegas. He flew to France and shoved a goose liver into the gullet of an enormous angler fish and brought it back. He knew that customs agents would never want to feel around in the gullet of a fish. With his precious foie gras he made a dish that wasn't on the menu, and food lovers swarmed the restaurant and greedily ate slightly seared foie gras in a wine reduction.

The love for delicious food. This love is analogous to that between men and women. Cooks and gourmets make ideal partners. The cook's purpose in life is to use food to make people happy, and the gourmet never stops thinking about good food. After I peeked through the crack in the pocket door last fall and saw Seok-ju and Se-yeon together, I started to think that people immersed in sex must be gourmets, too.

I sit at an old outdoor table at Marine Parade Laksa in the streets of Katong and focus on eating. The laksa, made with coconut milk and rice noodles and a handful of herbs, is rich and hot enough to burn the roof of my mouth. In this food paradise, the first thing I eat is the all-too-common two-dollar laksa. I think I might laugh. I wrap the noodles around my chopsticks and put them in my mouth. The thick rice noodles have a nice texture to them. I like rich, murky soup like this. This coconut smell. The scent of spices, the aroma of herbs. It's the smell of Singapore, where I first came with him, the old street we searched for, famished after walking in the East Coast Park near our hotel, the pastel houses and flowery tiles in Katong. If I turn the corner at that 7-Eleven I will see him standing awkwardly, tall and bent forward, like back then. If I walk three blocks I'll be at Katong Antique House—we will be preserved there like wax figures, him choosing a blouse for me, and me looking at china. First I'll finish this bowl. Then I'll go there, one more time. I slurp the soup.

The thousands of taste buds on my tongue wake up one after the other. Taste is the most pleasurable of all human senses. The happiness you get from eating can fill the absence of other pleasures. There's a time when all you can do is eat. When eating is the only way you can prove that you're still alive. Large raindrops splatter onto the table, signaling the imminent arrival of a squall.

To eat or not to eat. To love or not to love. That is the question for the five senses.

# CHAPTER 18

MEMORIES ARE LIKE A WINDMILL with sharp points, spinning in your heart, stabbing it. The more you dwell on them the more they spin, quicker and quicker. Will the edges eventually dull? Will such a day come? Am I actually longing for that day to come, or are the sharp points keeping me alive? My past stays with me no matter how much time flows by. It'll be good not to think about it, if only for three days. I bite my lip. Is there something I wouldn't be able to do unless I did it right now? I feel that something will change for me when I go home. I feel more trepidation than excitement. Here, all I do is eat at three different restaurants a day. My nervousness might be a sign that my subconscious is vibrantly alive. With that faint hope, I eat breakfast at Killiney Kopitiam near the Somerset MRT station—French toast with jam of kaya, made of coconut milk, eggs, and sugar. I sense saltiness before sweetness.

In the afternoon I'm supposed to attend the wine workshop at the Conrad. I buy two jars of homemade kaya jam and hop into a cab to Chinatown. It's hot and humid and it might rain again.

From a fruit stand I buy a green-tinged mango and a bright yellow Hawaiian papaya. I bypass exotic fruit like mangosteen, juicy and tart enough to be called the queen of fruit, little orange-colored bananas, and champedak, which is too smelly to bring into the hotel. I can make a sweet and light dessert by slicing the orange mango into thin slivers and shaving Gouda over it. Or these fruits would be perfect garnishes to honey-baked pumpkin. Mangosteen or champedak would be delicious with green-tea ice cream. Fruit is good on its own, but you can absorb more of its nutrients if you pair it with something else. Something is missing. I go into a Chinese bakery and buy a box of tarts. I don't know if he still likes these cookielike pies, made with plenty of pineapple sauce thickened for a long time on the stove. We've seen each other a few times since he left but we haven't eaten or drunk together. I don't want to believe his tastes have changed. One's sense of taste and smell do not change easily. I want to bake myself like a cake for him, or bake flour-salt dough into hard, salty, bracelet-shaped pretzels and cuff them to his wrists.

Chef was to join me at the wine workshop conducted by the wine expert Michel Rolland in the Conrad Hotel garden, but I don't see him. Kim and Choi would be on the sought-after gourmet safari, which takes you to three restaurants along the river. Rolland talks about Château Lebon Pasteur, which has notes of overripe plum and dried fig; it's made in Pomerol, his hometown. This wine might be ordinary for others but is special to him. According to Rolland, you eat from the lightest to the most intensely flavored dishes, but for wine you should drink from the heaviest to the lightest, the most flavorful to the most subtle. But that's not always true. Individual likes and dislikes are important in choosing wine, and the same is true for food. Rolland pours about half an inch of wine into glasses lined in a row on the table. Now it's time to taste. He raises his glass and says, This is the purest liquid in the world!

Ruby-red liquid dances in the glass, the color of condensed sunlight and wind, sophisticated and transparent. A question pops into my head. Pure water doesn't contain any molecules that draw out taste. So you can't taste something that is completely pure unless another element is added, whether it's a grain of salt or a few droplets of vinegar. Is the wine in my hand pure liquid or not?

On our last night in Singapore, our group decides to have dinner together at Seafood Center on the eastern shore. I stay back at the hotel alone. Just as a meal ends with coffee or ice cream, trips to Singapore always finish with seafood. This time I didn't feel like it, partly because of the wine I'd been drinking since the afternoon and the humidity sticking to my body like a wet cloth. My head hurts. It's not even eight o'clock when I return to my room after having a bowl of wonton soup at the third-floor Chinese restaurant. I sit in the tub with the water running, then emerge and lie down in the middle of the floor, water dripping off my body. Whatever energy I have drains out, as if someone were sprinkling kosher salt over my naked body. Three days is too long. To think of only one person, or to try as hard as I could not to think of him. *If you're sad just let yourself be sad.* I can't tell whether it's sadness or wistfulness or resignation pressing down on me. I want to sleep now. I want to enter into a deep and lengthy sleep, one I wouldn't wake from in the morning. Choi will be back soon. I don't have the energy to get in bed. I'm wilted, like hand-torn spinach. I manage to stretch my arm out and pull down the camel-colored blanket from my bed to cover myself. I feel warmth from my armpits, from the insides of my elbows, between my knees. Did I overindulge in eating and drinking? *Seok-ju, I'm freezing all of a sudden.*

I rub my eyes. A huge white horse stands in the middle of the room. I close my eyes, open them. A man wearing a white bathrobe stares down at me . . . Who is it? Like I'm looking through heavy fog dispersing slowly, I realize it's Chef. I'm about to raise myself up, but remember that I'm not wearing anything and that I'm not in a kitchen but a hotel room. I tug the blanket up to my chin. What time is it? Are they back from the seafood restaurant? Where's Choi and why is Chef here? Even though I'm lying down and Chef is just standing there, it's not awkward—it's as if we've done this before. All we've done was stand next to each other in a narrow kitchen, bumping into each other. I raise my neck with effort, to get up.

"Just stay there." His voice booms in the dark.

I'm surprised.

"Just five minutes."

I don't know what to say.

"I'll stay just five minutes and leave."

All of my vitality drains out. I hear cloth brushing against cloth. Chef is undoing his belt and taking off his bathrobe. Should I close my eyes? Even if I do it's not completely dark. I don't want to be nervous right now, like a fool. It'll be okay as long as I don't waver. Chef lies on top of me. He grips my hands holding the blanket and pulls them up toward my ears. I can feel his weight, his warmth, his breath on the other side of the thin blanket. Only our elbows to our fingers are actually touching, and his left cheek rests on mine. But it still feels like our entire bodies are touching. Nervous relief and sighs fill my chest. If I can't turn the clock back by five minutes, there's only one thing I can do. Lie quietly and wait for time to pass.

"Breathe." His voice sounds so loud.

". . . Okay."

"I'm not going to do anything."

*I know.*

"So please just stay still."

*Yes, that's what I'm doing.*

"I'm going to go soon."

*I don't want to ruin our friendship of thirteen years, formed one drop at a time.* "You're too heavy."

He moves a leg off me. It's easier to breathe. Chef is the kind of person who would forgo pleasure that might later bring guilt. We have to be able to eat toast comfortably at the hotel café tomorrow morning, as if nothing happened. We have to be able to complain that the coffee is too weak or that it's flavorless. We lie there, looking at each other, not saying a thing, listening to faraway sounds. The night around me is dreamy and dizzy and too hot, like when you eat too much fermented mango.

"Every time I look at you I'm reminded of her."

I stay silent.

"I used to be alive because of her."

Is he talking about his ex-wife or his dead daughter? I've known him for a long time but I know next to nothing about his private life. But I wish he wouldn't say that I remind him of either of them.

"I didn't have the chance to love her fully. I didn't have enough time."

He's talking about his daughter. "You can say anything you want."

He's surprised.

"Because we're leaving tomorrow. We're going home. Don't do it there. Don't be this close to me there."

". . . Okay."

I want to nod but I can't move. His face is pressing down and his shoulder is flattening and his leg is pushing down, his entire body smashed on mine.

"I wanted to remember her growing up. When I gave her baths I used to put her heel into my mouth. Babies don't have much of a heel before they walk. It's just a soft and squishy foot. It would move around in my mouth. A shock would go through

113

my entire body—she was alive, and so was I. When it felt heavier in my mouth I knew—Oh, she's grown this much. After she turned one, I couldn't even put it in my mouth. She was too big. Then she started walking. I felt a loss but I liked to see her walking and jumping and running with her heels that were starting to harden. I was happy that I was alive."

I'm quiet. Four days after the five-year-old was kidnapped, she was found in a manhole near their house. "What did it taste like?"

Chef doesn't know what I'm talking about.

"Her heel."

". . . Sweet. Really sweet and tender."

"Like a green grape?"

"No, it was purer and cleaner."

We're quiet for a moment.

"I've been to Dohoku," I say.

"Right."

"It's famous for its horse meat. It's amazing, the marbling of the bloodred and white, showing through the paper-thin slices of meat. I put it in my mouth and the juices of the meat welled between the crevices of my teeth. Like a horse was slowly walking into my mouth. It filled me up. Was it like that?"

"Yeah, that's what it was like."

"Right."

". . . No matter where you go, you can't find that taste."

"You probably can't."

"Yeah, it's the taste of something that doesn't exist in this world."

"A special taste."

"I wanted to re-create that taste."

We're silent for a moment.

*Are you crying?* My cheek is wet, warm. It's as if we've touched the deepest parts of each other, the parts that are untouchable.

"I have someone like that, too. Someone who makes me feel like I'm living."

Chef doesn't say a word.

"I didn't have enough time with him either."

"Don't. Don't do that to yourself anymore."

"If it were easy it wouldn't be love."

Chef is quiet.

"Don't tell me that's not true."

"I won't."

"You know how there's a taste that can't be substituted by anything else in the world? There are people that can't be substituted by any other person."

"Yeah, that's true."

"This is enough for now."

"Yeah, this is enough."

"Yeah."

We stay silent again.

He unglues his face from my cheek. I watch him letting go of my hands, lifting his shoulders, slowly moving his legs away from me. I close my eyes. Because if I were to see his body, I might continue to recall this vivid sensation, which feels like a hot root pushing through me.

"But you," Chef says, slipping into his bathrobe, about to step away. "You're so small." His voice brims with heartbreaking emotion and the love he couldn't give in its entirety, as if he were talking to his daughter, frozen in youth.

I hear the door shut.

My heart hasn't wavered, I whisper into the darkness. But somewhere, something in my being has bent, as easily as a grapevine. I turn over on my side. My body heats up, as if someone has put his mouth around my heel.

115

# CHAPTER 19

H UMANS AND DOGS yearn for attention and love. While humans worry about what others think of them, dogs are more interested in your behavior. Dogs react differently if the other person is more dominant. But if a dog doesn't get his way, he will gradually begin to use threats, even if he's the most well trained dog. Paulie, though confident and wise and graceful, has begun to think up ways to threaten me.

One day after it rains, Paulie plods into the living room from the yard. Mud is covering his beautiful golden-red fur and he smells musty. With mud caking everything but his eyes, Paulie barks once as if to tell me that he rolled in the mud on purpose, jumps onto the sofa, then leaps onto the butcher block. What are you doing, Paulie? I yell. Paulie glances at me and continues on, as if he wouldn't even consider stopping until he gets what he wants. I don't budge. I sit on a kitchen stool, not looking at him, pretending to read the magazine in front of me. A dog's eyes are different from a human's, but all eyes are sensitive to movement. I toss the magazine aside and stand up.

Paulie, hesitating, lies down, his front paws placed side by side. Seok-ju doesn't come to see Paulie anymore. Of course, he doesn't come to see me, either. *I want what you want, Paulie. But he doesn't want what we want. You should understand that by now.* I gently stroke his head to soothe him. Only the odor of the mud reverberates in the room. I push my hand deeper into Paulie's coat. His scent's completely evaporated now. *You can't wait obediently anymore, right, Paulie? You use your nose to understand and remember the world. Right?* We're having a conversation. A depressed dog, like a depressed person, shows physical symptoms—erratic behavior and eyes so cloudy that he wouldn't be able to recognize his owner. We must be suffering from the same illness, and I think we communicate as best we can about it. But that turns out to be an incorrect belief.

A few days later, when I come home from work, Paulie is rolling a dead cat around like a ball, and when he sees me staring at him, a hand to my mouth, he plops down on top of it. As if to say, I've always liked smelly, squishy things. When I manage to pull Paulie away and stick him in the tub, he latches onto my neck. It's not really a bite—he puts pressure on my neck with his muzzle the way he does when he pushes my knee, but we aren't playing catch or wrestling like the other times. I feel a sudden terror. Dogs show their unhappiness with their mouths. If they're pushed into a corner, they bite, even if it happens to be their owner. Paulie is agitated. I need to be calm. I have to be more attentive to his needs. Even though I've already turned on the water, I put the showerhead down on the floor as if to show him that I mean no harm. Whether you're a dog or a human, if your needs are unfulfilled, you will feel like attacking. Is this what I'm really afraid of?

Paulie is still baring his teeth, revealing his beastly side. I turn off the water and slide down to the floor. We sit in a puddle, our bottom halves wet, staring at each other. *You can't do this, Paulie.* I grab the scruff of his neck and raise him up, glaring into his eyes. A bite to the neck is a challenge to hierarchy. I sharply slap his skinny nose. If he continues to misbehave, the only thing left to do is stop feeding him. No. I lose my resolve and drop my hand. I shake my head. I have to think about what's best for this old dog. What would be the best for Paulie? As if waiting for a new challenge, Paulie breathes hard, looking seriously into my eyes. I turn away from him in a firm and exaggerated gesture so that he will understand it, even with his failing eyesight. I want to say, Now we're over.

I need to be firm. I don't have the right to keep a dog when all I do is just look at him. I have no right to keep Paulie. Paulie is here not because he wants to stay with me but because he doesn't have a choice. A dog doesn't stay by his owner's side in the face of danger out of love or loyalty. He's merely waiting for what happens next. Humans think it's because the dog loves his owner, but a dog is only a dog. I grab Paulie in an embrace. Paulie is only a dog. He's merely his dog. Okay, I'll bring you back to him, I whisper into Paulie's ear. *So you can stop being like this, Paulie.* The perfect place for this dog is the house he, Paulie's first owner, is living in. This is the last thing I can do for Paulie.

Before I send Paulie to him, to them, I realize something: Even the most well-trained dog will not move the way we want him to, and a dog feels terror, desire, curiosity, anger, satisfaction, hesitation, and loss just like us. A human instinctively wants to cuddle and protect a smaller and weaker being, furry and soft, with big eyes and a round head. And when Paulie is not acting up, he is so beautiful and gentle and loyal. Even though I know she can't stand dogs, I dial her number, which I still know by heart, in the hopes that she will feel maternal toward him.

# MAY

*The fourth rule is, to have all ingredients and materials
necessary for the preparation of your dishes ready
and handy before you commence cooking, so that
nothing need be hurriedly done . . .*

—Henriette Davidis' Practical Cook Book

# CHAPTER 20

I N THE SUBWAY CAR on line three, I see a woman holding a large globe. I am going to work two hours earlier than usual, to meet the delivery of a big, twenty-five-kilogram perch and ten kilograms of blue crab from Wando Island. The woman looks straight ahead, her overstuffed duffel bag leaning on the seat next to her and the colorful globe on her lap, perhaps on her way to somewhere far. It's unexpected to see a globe in an uncrowded subway car, and I stare at it as if I've never seen such a thing. When you spin a globe it feels like you can go anywhere in the world—the world is as small as your kitchen. But just as you can never see the Southern Cross from the North Pole, you can never see the other side of the world. You can leave whenever you want, but a time may come when staying here is beyond your willpower. The plastic globe sways on its axis with every shake of the subway car.

I close my eyes and pretend to be asleep. My stop is announced. I open my eyes. The woman is no longer across from me. Neither is the globe, which looked heavy for its size. I manage to slip out just before the doors close. I pause momentarily while climbing the stairs. I can't recall whether the woman was holding a globe, or a newborn baby swaddled in a colorful blanket, or a lapdog. Was I dozing in the early-morning subway? I keep walking, thinking it would have been better to see someone holding a big, slightly cracked melon instead. At least you can eat a melon. I haven't been able to fall into deep slumber all spring. When reading a book or drinking herbal tea doesn't help, I go into the yard and pace, barefoot, watching the sunrise. Now even Paulie isn't there, Paulie, whose warm tongue used to lick my face.

The gigantic fish is splayed across the butcher block, dripping water. It's so fresh that I think its eyes will fly open, tail flopping. A century ago the perch wouldn't have arrived in an ice-filled Styrofoam box but in a clay jar of honey. Tension flits in the air among the six cooks who gather around the fish with their knives. Last month, I decided not to handle fish for a while. I feel warmer than usual and my palms sweat—the worst hands with which to touch fish. I've never been this hot before. I don't know why this is happening. I gaze down at my palms. Is it because I'm completely alone? I shake my head. These thoughts only make my palms warmer. It'll get better when the seasons change.

It feels like warm—and cold—liquid is seeping out of my body, like juice from cutting a ripe peach. I can't do anything but wait for time to pass. If you want to pursue something, it means you have desire. There's something I want to grab firmly with these two hands. I stand in front of the large oven that reflects my face and whisper: *The hours I wait with desire will certainly be mysterious.*

It's disappointing that I can't handle the perch—the tiger of the sea—but I step back. A fish this size has a lot of flesh and

allows you to bring out all kinds of flavors. One hand support-
ing my chin, I glance at Chef, wondering how this one will be
prepared. I think of Chef every time I look at a perch, just as
I'm reminded of a cow or yellow paprika whenever I see Mun-
ju. What do people think when they look at me? Do they asso-
ciate me with a vegetable or a fish? Chef picks up a knife, slides
it along the dorsal fin, and slits the body open. Everyone, even
Manager Park, gathers around the fish, curiosity gleaming in
their eyes. Chef will carefully divide the body, cheeks, collar,
stomach, liver, small intestines, and gills and distribute them to
the staff. Then he will tell them to make a dish out of it—
homework. This is how Chef uses a perch, as expensive as a
whole calf. Another reason you don't leave Nove once you start
cooking here. A few years ago I parboiled the liver of a perch in
salted water before stewing it in garlic sauce. Chef's opinion
was that my concoction was fine, but that it didn't show enough
imagination and tasted one-dimensional.

The kitchen becomes busy all of a sudden. While the others
work on the perch, I take charge of marinated blue crab for the
staff meal. Shellfish live underwater and breathe through their
gills, periodically shedding their shells as they grow. The time to
get the plumpest and sweetest shellfish is right before they
shed. Blue crabs in May are packed with eggs—they don't taste
as good after they lay eggs. Chef makes the soy sauce used for
the marinade. Soy sauce is the one condiment I'm not very comfortable using. If Grandmother were still alive, I could learn
from her. Grandmother used a pear reduction to satisfy all the
need for sweetness in her cooking, and when she made marinated crabs she used pear juice instead of sugar for the soy sauce.
Worm-mottled pears, old pears, frozen pears—they all turned
into sweet, clear pear reduction when they passed through
Grandmother's hands. Chef believes that a young person can't

handle soy sauce. By the time I learn how to make and handle it, I may no longer be young. My wish is that I will still be in this kitchen.

The darkest soy sauce, like the darkest caviar and olives, is the best. Soy sauce has to be black and have a tongue-seducing aroma, but it can't be overly viscous and you should take care to use only the appropriate amount. The squirming crabs are piled into a nickel bowl. One even lurches and claws its way to the top. If they were lobsters, we would immediately snip the muscles in their claws. Lobsters, the most belligerent of shellfish, eat each other when they are kept in a confined space. We don't do anything to the crabs yet, though, because the flavor suffers when a knife touches living crabs. Now I should pour the soy sauce over the crabs. After boiling and cooling the sauce, I dip a finger into the liquid and stick it in my mouth, rolling it around on my tongue. Sour and salty and sweet and profoundly weighty, like when I take a sip of good wine. I pour the sauce over the live crabs. They writhe as if in protest. Now all I have to do is wait until they die, then trim the claws.

# CHAPTER 21

A STRANGE THING HAPPENS on Thursday afternoon. I take a walk down the hill near the Shilla Hotel before dinner service. Suddenly a black flock of pigeons rises up in front of me. Dust and pollen fly into my face, and as I pull my hands out of my pockets to shield my eyes, I see through my fingers a pigeon flying swiftly toward my foot. My foot pauses in midair as the pigeon rushes forward and swoops onto it, swallowing it whole. With no time to regain my balance, I take a tumble in the middle of the street. Rolling on the downward slope, I realize it wasn't a pigeon but a black plastic bag. But that's after I've already fallen. For a while I lie there on my stomach without moving. I must have broken something, I think. My cheek, which scraped along the sidewalk, starts to burn. Two pedestrians try to help me up. I'm okay, I say, pushing their hands away, thinking, I hope I hurt my ankle, not my wrists. I sit up slowly and flex my wrists. If I hurt my hands, I won't be able to cook anymore, or even go into the kitchen. I won't be able to do anything, either at home or at Nove. This has to be more horrific than being alone. My wrists seem fine. I don't feel any pain. I get up and rotate each of my ankles. They're fine, too. It's odd. It was as if someone yanked on my ankles, yet not a single part of me was hurt. I fell only a few seconds ago but it seems like a hallucination. But the black plastic bag that enveloped my left foot and my sore cheek are proof that it wasn't. It happened in a split second. My foot was held up to take a step, and the black plastic bag, tossed by the wind, fell to the ground as if carefully planned, heading toward my shoe with its opening facing me. The scene remains in my head as if I pressed the pause button. It happened in the blink of an eye but I couldn't avoid it.

I'm glad I didn't get hurt, but I'm dogged by an ominous feeling that I'm the butt of an unpleasant joke. That night I receive two complaints about my food. Once it's too salty and the other time the food isn't seasoned at all. What's wrong with you today? Manager Park says unpleasantly. I don't go with the group to eat truffle dishes at the InterContinental. Recently the hotel has become the center of talk among gourmets because it imported twenty kilograms of fresh truffles from France for the first time ever. It's a large amount, worth around forty million won. I asked the head manager of the hotel, who is close to Chef, to get me a truffle, even if it's as small as a clove of garlic. Not believing that I tripped over a black plastic bag, I cluck as if someone is watching. It was stupid to think that the bag was a pigeon. If there were two of me, I would pat the shoulder of the other me in sympathy. *It's probably because you haven't been sleeping well.* When you're alone for a long time, you learn how to think of yourself as separate from even yourself.

I'm tired of hoping he will come by and waiting for the phone to ring. With even Paulie gone, there's nothing left that connects me to him. I lie on the living room couch and look up at the spiral staircase leading to the second floor, giving in to my imagination. I imagine receiving his phone call; I imagine him coming to see me, sitting with him at the table to eat, and making love with him after we've slowly peeled off our clothing. But here I am lying in the dark listlessly, my ribs sticking out.

I get up and open the fridge. I take out a head of cabbage, thick, big, heavy. I rip off some leaves and wash and drop them into boiling water to make broth. I've heard the story of a blind person recovering his sight after washing his eyes with cabbage broth—possible only in legend. But we did exactly that three years ago. I placed at his bedside a bundle of tetterwort I'd collected from the hospital grounds and waited every night, fervently, for him to produce tears. It was the hardest time, he said once in a quiet voice, remembering. And he gripped my hand, which he was holding, even harder. Where did those times go?

I place the lid on the pot and balance over it the ladle I had been holding. The broth of a boiled cabbage is effective in treating alcoholism as well as insomnia. If I can't fall asleep I'll be unable to tell bean sprouts from mung-bean sprouts, confuse flounder with stingray, and continue to trip over plastic bags and fall. A sour smell wafts up, the smell of cabbage.

Cabbage is born from tears. When Dionysus arrived in Trachia, Likourgos led his army to capture the god. Gaia, the goddess of the earth, cast a spell on Likourgos, who went crazy and, confusing his son Drias for a grapevine, took his sword and cut him in two. Adonis then captured and tortured him, ripping his body apart. Cabbage sprouted from the sand where Likourgos' tears dropped. Even now, farmers don't plant cabbage near grapevines because bees might transfer the smell of cabbage onto the grapes. Cabbage contains sulfur, so it stinks when you boil it. People are most sensitive to bitterness. I down the hot cabbage broth and get into bed and pull the covers over my head.

What would grow from this place where my tears have dropped? It would be better to think about something else. Something more interesting and sensual and specific. Something I can fall asleep to with a smile on my face.

Coffee and bread
Butter and jam
Ham and Emmentaler
Truffles and foie gras
Mayonnaise and cooled roast chicken
Melon and Parma ham
Caviar and vodka
Pea porridge and honey
Fried cod and garlic
Spinach and roast duck
Shrimp and curry
Scallops and pasta
Mussels and white wine
Calf brains and butter sauce

I feel myself loosening up, as if a spoonful of something delicious has just entered my mouth. I understand how appetite and hunger and thirst and deprivation expand one's palate. I smack my lips and sink one step further into sleep. If I were a fish, I would be a small, flat, fresh, sparkling, silver-gray turbot. One that has firm flesh and delivers a good bite, best when you crunch down on it whole including the bones—one you can eat in small pieces. If I had to be a shellfish, I'd like to be a scallop, floating deep in the ocean. I don't want to be an oyster even though it's snow white and brimming with sweet brine. An oyster lives its life changing from male to female and back again. I like the oyster's spiraling, intricate shell, which is harder to shuck than you might think. I don't want to be a starfish, either.

A starfish slinks past shellfish, leaving behind only an empty shell—a chilling sight. Even though sea urchin and sea cucumbers are fragrant and expensive, I don't want to be a spineless organism like them. I'll stick with being a scallop.

If I were a fruit, I would want to be a ripe avocado, with a hard stone hidden in the middle of soft, silken flesh. Any fruit would be fine, really, except an orange, a hardy-looking but sensitive fruit that turns even if it's jostled a little. Then again, I do need bright sunshine, wind, and adequate moisture, just like an orange. What about a cherry? It's not overly juicy but it has a beautiful red color, like a miniature sun. A banana would be fine too. A banana tree has no branches but is made of large leaves. A smaller banana is sweeter. It's a unique fruit; nobody knows how it came into being. The tree produces only one bunch of bananas at a time, but that bunch is made of hundreds of clusters of fruit. I think I can fall deeper into slumber.

In my dream I'm surrounded by fragrant fruit and I'm conjuring up various foods but I can't taste any of them. In dreams, taste and smell affect your soul in a minimal way. But the other senses are as acute as when your eyes are open, so if you weep in your dreams you'll wake up to a wet pillow. In the dream I am not a turbot or a scallop or a cherry or a banana. I'm an oyster gone sour, my juices dried up. I'm placed on a hot fire. A bad oyster should be grilled with butter and sprinkled with nutmeg. I feel pain, as if a sharp knife is being shoved into my closed shell. I wipe my eyes and push back the covers with a jolt. The phone. I think the phone is ringing. I grab the receiver.

". . . It's me."

I nod.

"Were you still up?"

"I was having a bad dream."

"I'm sorry it's so late."

"That's okay."

"I was debating whether to call. And it kept getting later."

"It's okay."

A phone call you wait for never comes. Except now. My heart pounds. *Tell me that you called because you were wondering how I was doing. That you missed me. And say one more thing. That you want to come back. Tell me you called to see if you could come back. Then all of this can end. Quietly.* I grip the phone tighter. I want to remember this moment forever. What is this love? Is it gold or a diamond, or maybe a truffle? This love is what everyone wants but can't make, just like gold and diamonds and truffles. I gleam in a sprightly green, a spring asparagus.

"I have to tell you something."

". . . Yeah."

"I don't know how to say it."

"Yes. Come back."

". . . What?"

"Come back."

"That's not what this is about."

"It's okay. Just say it. Say whatever it is."

"Paulie, he . . . he died."

I hear metal grating against metal. "Wh-what?"

"I know it's hard to believe, but he died."

I hunch my shoulders. "What are you talking about?"

"Today—no, it's already yesterday."

"Is Paulie—is he very sick?"

". . . No, he's dead."

"Are you joking?"

"No."

"Tell me you're joking!" I growl.

"It's the truth."

"Say it again."

"Paulie's dead."

I'm silent.

"Are you listening to me?"

"What did you two do to him?"

"It was an accident."

". . . Did he die? Or did you kill him? Tell me."

"I told you, it was an accident."

I can't speak.

He says one more time that Paulie is dead, his voice hoarse.

# CHAPTER 22

*R*ESTAURANT—the word originates from the French verb *restaurer*, "to restore to a former state," and until the eighteenth century it referred to a nutritious and invigorating soup. It was only after that that the word changed to signify a place that provided meals. The man who opened the world's first restaurant was a Frenchman named Boulanger. But the gourmets of the world remember not Boulanger but Beauvilliers, a restaurateur and chef. When a customer entered his restaurant, Beauvilliers would take one glance at him and tell him what he should avoid and what he should eat, then personally prepare dishes that couldn't be found anywhere else. He became famous not only for his cooking skills and the special attention he paid everyone but also for his extensive memory, which allowed him to recognize an occasional customer twenty years later. French newspapers mourned him when he died in 1820, writing about his life at length.

When I was in cooking school, Chef preferred to teach common sense or the history of ingredients or the behavior of cooks rather than how to cook. And even now he remembers what customers ate and drank on their first visits, which impresses them. Even the way he conveys his knowledge is natural and subtle. This isn't so much a sales gimmick as his conviction as a chef, as the owner of Nove. Whenever he does it, Manager Park shakes his head, jaw dropping, and says, I still have a long way to go! Chef would have been Beauvilliers had he lived in the nineteenth century. Customers keep returning to the restaurant—to regain strength or for a special dinner or because they don't have time to cook or don't want to.

The restaurant is fully booked for every meal in May because of its numerous holidays—Coming-of-Age Day, Parents' Day, Children's Day, Teachers' Day. The kitchen becomes chaotic. In May, Chef reminds us during the morning staff meeting that we shouldn't use perfume, scented lotions, or shampoo. This reminder kicks off the busiest month and the start of summer. When seven cooks, sometimes including Chef, are stuck together like wooden chopsticks in the small kitchen, you can smell cigarettes and each other's sweat and even bodily fluids discharged during the previous night. Smell, especially that of food, has weighty particles, and when it's hot they can't rise and end up hovering near the bottom. It's also around this time that we raise our voices when even small accidents happen. In May you can't take off work except for your regular days off. But even if it was my day off I would have headed into work after receiving that phone call yesterday. I don't want to rest, not for even a day. I come to work earlier than anyone else and do chores that aren't mine, prepping ingredients and going to the market and bustling about as if I'll become frozen if I stop for five minutes. Every time I move, I hear my disjointed bones rattling in my body.

Before, I used to look at the world as if a piece of glass separated me from it. If the glass was cracked or broken, the other side of the glass would look like barely fitting puzzle pieces even if everything was perfect. The glass I look through now has thousands of irreparable spidery cracks in it. If you don't give up and you wish with all your strength that things go back to the way they were, maybe it could happen despite the cracks. But that's not common. I know when it's time to give up.

When I was seven years old, I was always home alone while Grandmother was at work and Uncle at school. I went into the kitchen and brought out a spoon and started to dig in the corner of the yard. When the spoon became bent and unusable, I burrowed with a ladle. I went to the well across the yard and drew water and poured it into the hole. The water disappeared silently into the dirt but I dug wider and deeper and poured in more water. I went back and forth between the well and the hole until the sun went down. I thought I would be able to make a pond. But water didn't remain in the hole even though I poured and poured—it just vanished into the dirt. I continued to trot between the well and the hole for the satisfaction I got in that short moment—the instant before the water completely melted into the ground. But then I stopped. I realized I wouldn't be able to make a pond no matter how hard I tried. It's now time to stop pouring water into the ground. I make this decision and discover I'm changed. A subtle but powerful feeling.

The first change is a realization that I am no longer alone. Even when I'm lying in the dark by myself, I now sense other beings hovering near me. It isn't just me living in this house, but unfinished love and my dejection and anger and dead Paulie, and their miraculous presence feels as real as my fingernails digging into my hand. The second change is that I'm now more obsessed with cooking, like the Roman gourmets and their cherished chefs, who wanted to put all things wonderful or special or new or majestic or strange or scary-looking on the table. The cooks back then knew only how to bake or boil, but I understand how a few drops of pomegranate juice can transform a dish. The third change is that with these first two revelations, my sense of taste has become ever more sensitive and sharp, my imagination richer. When I got my ears pierced and walked into the street in the middle of winter, I became one large ear. All sensation and pain were concentrated in my ears. My entire body vanished and I floated around the winter streets, just two giant ears. It's that same feeling. Everything about me disappears and I'm only a pink tongue. This is the time to grow into a truly good chef. I see an increase in customers who specially order my dishes. People come to restaurants for various reasons but everyone really wants the same thing: a delicious meal. A meal that satisfies their tongues. A meal that brings a smile at its close. All of these customers are gourmets—intelligent, sensitive, with good appetites and acute senses. A good appetite no longer is the subject of condemnation or avoidance as it was during the Middle Ages; rather, it's the height of beauty and nature and enjoyment. I am surrounded by those with appetites, which triggers the desire for taste, for a physical sensation. I want to create the perfect meal.

Slicing turbot in half is an insult to the fish, and it's rude to have a mediocre cook handle foie gras. Tonight we need to pay the most attention to the table of Mr. Choe, the owner of Mido, who helped Chef become the owner of Ristorante when he was head chef, before Chef renamed it Nove. Chef will cook the entrée, as he always does when Mr. Choe comes in, and I'm to make the second antipasto: asparagus and foie gras. After we returned from Singapore, we became something like confidants to one another. Was it that we each saw the other's true face that night, normally hidden behind many masks?

I hurry. I take five hundred grams of foie gras, hardened by a sprinkling of salt. It's dark red with a sheen and it's firm, like the tongue of a calf. It's a fresh, good-quality liver. But I smile bitterly. I can't eat foie gras anymore after I learned how geese were farmed. A cook should eat everything, but even a cook balks at eating certain things, delicious or not. I know cooks who can't eat poultry or those who can't eat fish with teeth, like stingray. I can eat crustaceans feeding on spoiled flesh and Milanese sausages stuffed with chopped pig brains, but goose liver is a different story.

A goose hatches in the spring and fattens during the fall. The liver is the best part of a goose. The goose is fed only vegetables in the warm darkness until it's fat enough, and to make the liver even more tender, to make it the best product, for twenty days it's fed only dried figs softened in water. A goose has a strong immune system and it's fairly easy to pull its beak open and force-feed it, allowing for less manpower—but these days, to eliminate even this work, the part in the brain that regulates appetite is removed. All you have to do is paralyze the goose, connect electrodes to the base of its brain, and turn on the electricity. Afterward you cage the goose under artificial lighting and it continues to eat, deep in its hallucinations. Within a week the goose is as fat as if it's been fed for a month, and so is its liver. If you take out its eyes, you can fatten it up even more.

I rush out of the kitchen and run into the bathroom. It's as if an eyeless, hallucinating goose is pacing behind me, eating endlessly under artificial lights. I vomit. A sourness rushes up. If you give a goose an egg-shaped rock, it will nestle and protect it without any suspicion. It will look after anything as one of its own, even a cloth doll. Geese develop a continuous attachment to the object they first encounter—the imprinting phenomenon is especially strong in a goose. A gosling develops an unconditional attachment with the first moving object it sees. It could be its mother or a sibling, a cat or a dog, a person or a motorcycle or a tractor. Even if it is the wrong focus of attention, the goose can't put an end to its unrequited courting. I throw up once more and press the toilet lever with irritation.

You don't have the right to handle foie gras if you're imagining quacking geese following a tractor around. You're a useless artist who has lost all objectivity toward your model. I wash my hands with soap several times and return to the kitchen. I place the foie gras in the center of the dish, then place cold steamed asparagus on a diagonal. I once thought that if love were tangible, it would be a truffle or asparagus. Things that push through the ground. I shake my head. Asparagus has to be cut and eaten when it sprouts in the spring, while it's tender. If you leave it alone, it quickly turns into a large, fuzzy leaf, growing into a thick pole too big to grip. Asparagus continues to grow even after you cut it, though slowly. If it's true that I've changed, my thoughts on the food and my fingers on the butcher block will be even colder, even more detached. Unlike the kitchen, the world is filled with things I can't control.

I spear a leftover piece of foie gras and hand the fork to Chef, asking with my eyes how it is. Chef puts it into his mouth and chews, nods once. I put the plate on the pass. Manager Park comes and quickly takes it away—foie gras has to be eaten warm. I'm done for now. I think I have time to take a five-minute break, but I double back just as I'm about to leave the kitchen. If black caviar is the dream of gourmets, foie gras was born from human desire and pleasure. Horatius once said that liver is the seat of passion, the home to sensual love and wrath. I stick the last piece of foie gras into my mouth and hide it under my tongue. I press my lips together and push it down.

# CHAPTER 23

•

W HEN I WATCH gorgeous women mingling, I think I can understand Seok-ju. He wouldn't have been able to tear his eyes off Se-yeon, a yellow daffodil in dark soil, standing with her head tilted down as if to convey that she didn't want to be noticed in a crowd of people. He would have met her gaze. There's nothing shocking about a young architect with a promising future falling in love with a beautiful former model. There just shouldn't have been a woman called K between them. The architect should have met the model before he met K. Because he was the first man that K had loved, he—they— should have been more understanding, should have been more cautious about their love. There are rules even when you wrench a toy away from a young child. I nod along to the soft techno music that sounds like sorrowful weeping. The people who have gathered today for *Wine & Food*'s ten-year anniversary party are mostly owners of the best restaurants or companies that import wine or cheese. But there may be even more models and celebrities and stylists and designers. Every time I meet the eyes of the tall and thin and beautiful, wearing great clothes and a mist of strong perfume, I feel my pupils widen as if I'm a man looking at gorgeous women.

From the bar, a woman I know waves at me. She's a news anchor who often comes to Nove and eats only the crusts when she eats bread because she's afraid of gaining weight. I almost don't recognize Chef, who's sitting next to her. He doesn't like to come to these events. If Mun-ju hadn't asked us to cater it, he might not have come at all. After discussions with the magazine, we decided to go with scent as the party's theme. You can't neglect the preferences of the people attending the event you cater. My strategy in catering events is to put out a few memorable and special dishes that are light but filling. An adjective hides behind the word "scent"—sensual. Sensuality triggers a desire to touch and eat, awakening the senses. The sense of smell is powerful, the sense most closely linked to taste. From a cook's point of view, the scent of food is a necessity for skinny women who avoid eating. Tonight many known gourmets have come to the party. It's important to sate them and tickle their taste buds, but you shouldn't completely satisfy them. If they're satisfied, they'll want something better. You have to leave some expectation for the next course. It's important to make food that sustains the appetite. Gourmets are capricious, preferring to eat out and be critics instead of cooking at home, wanting to experience even more flavors and desiring satisfaction from food that doesn't exist. They are finicky and demanding and temperamental, but I need them.

For the first dish of the buffet, I have prepared oysters. It's not the peak season for oysters because this is when they breed, but at least it's not June or July, when they lay eggs. There's no need to make many appetizers. It's sufficient to use sight and smell to lightly awaken the appetite before the actual meal. I place lemon-spritzed oysters on the half shell between ice carvings surrounding a large fountain of ice. Fresh oysters emit a marine-fresh smell, and the lemon juice hints at tropical fruit ripened in the sun. I also have a ceviche of olive-oil-marinated turbot garnished with chopped shallots and caviar that goes well with the white wine we're serving with the oysters. It's an appetizer that will turn heads: the white turbot, light-purple shallots, the pink fig sauce, the shiny black caviar.

The mains are salmon with scallop sauce and rib eye with sauce périgueux. I purposely don't make enough for everyone. Even if you give it out for free, if there's too much food it doesn't look pricey or fresh. For those who will be coming late, I prepare light bite-size sandwiches, canapés of cheese, caviar, and paprika, cinnamon-sprinkled ravioli filled with watercress and melon, and dark-red cherries. And also dessert, which can never be omitted. The colors of my dishes are varied and gorgeous and sensual, evocative of the theme of scent. The chocolate at the end of the buffet table contains over 90 percent cacao. It's chocolate that's almost a drug—even a tiny bite will intoxicate. I sprinkle powder from this chocolate onto ice cream made from cheese and fresh cream. It would have been very expensive if Mun-ju hadn't gotten the vendors to sponsor the event.

I got a present for Mun-ju, a black vase shaped like a squat candlestick decorated with red roses and ivy, which she placed in the middle of the buffet table. Amid the warm, silken food and the flowers and the sparkling, jewel-like crystal stemware, the guests eat and drink and talk and laugh and hug and blow away smoke and dance in a way that makes even the smallest movements look erotic. Mun-ju, wearing a breezy chiffon dress, is acting the hostess, flushed, mingling. She winks when our eyes meet, to say, It's perfect, it's a smash! Everyone is laughing and everyone is giving off a fragrance. In the center is the table draped with a white cloth and on top are my dishes, the product of several days of planning and preparation.

143

I break away from the crowd and lean against the wall and start drinking cold, salty margaritas. It's fine to get a little tipsy on a day like this. My lips burn, soaked in alcohol and salt. I push a canapé into my mouth. I pop the caviar with the tip of my tongue. I feel sweetness, saltiness. Even though I put just a morsel into my mouth, I sink completely into the caviar's unique and vivid taste, as if I'm a butterfly with taste organs on its front legs, sensing sweetness if one leg touches nectar. The music continues to play and it's as if the party is never going to end. I didn't eat a bite all evening because I was cooking. I should eat something. I fetch another margarita and down it quickly.

I think I smell a burning cube of sugar. Is it the scent of a violet? The fragrance that blooms disappears, then opens. The smell of Se-yeon's perfume. Marjoram. Is she here? Midsniff, I open my eyes wide. The anchor who was at the bar is swishing by me. Her perfume swirls in the air like a long breath and dissipates slowly. The intense scent lingers like the fluids left on after-sex bedsheets, the smell that captivated him. The fragrance throws me off balance, appearing in an unexpected place. Do I give off a scent, too? I stick my hand, still wet and swollen, into my pocket. The most sensual of aromas is the essence of a young raven fed only boiled eggs for forty days, then killed and preserved in myrtle and almond oil. The smell that all women want to give off and that all men want. Musk is altogether too common, but it excites people instinctually. In Elizabethan times, women slipped a peeled apple between their arms and, when it was soaked in sweat, gave it to their lovers to smell. Smell is the longest-lasting memory. People stay and go, but smell transcends time. The smell of an apple soaked in sweat, the scent of a raven killed after a diet of boiled eggs. I want to be like these extreme pheromones, creating explosions of taste. I don't want to be helpless, stumbling like this.

"Haven't you had too much to drink today?" Chef comes and sits next to me.

"Didn't you say I could take tomorrow off?"

"You're going to burn out if you work like this."

I feel him looking at me. I pour some Almaviva, a Chilean wine, into his glass and pick mine up. Almaviva is named after the character in *The Barber of Seville*, popular at festivities. The wine glides gently down my throat—multiple layers of velvet. I don't think I'm drunk yet. "Those people, they look really happy."

"It's a party. There's wine and food."

"Yes. Weddings always end with a reception, and there's cake for birthdays."

"Because it's social."

"What is?"

"Food."

I'm quiet.

"Like you need food when you do business."

I nod. I think I know what he's talking about. Like people make offerings for religious ceremonies.

"Is everything okay with you these days?" Chef asks.

"Everything's fine."

"You don't have to tell me if you don't want to."

"It's just—I can't sleep very well."

". . . About Mido."

"Yes?"

"They decided to hold their meetings at the restaurant from now on."

I'm confused.

"It's because of you. The food was good that night."

I'm quiet.

"Good job."

". . . Thank you."

"I just wanted to say that." Chef looks away, toward the front of the room. I pick up my wineglass again and take a deep gulp. Chef complimented me for the first time a little before I quit Nove, four years ago. The first time I heard praise from the mentor who taught me for more than ten years. This is the second time. The wine becomes hotter and heavier. Am I getting drunk? It doesn't matter even if I am. It doesn't matter even if I want to cry. *Good job.* His voice echoes in my ears. My chest is burning up. I'm not happy. I bow my head. As if to admit to myself for the first time how much power Chef has over me.

"Paulie's dead."

Chef is stunned.

Seok-ju came by two nights ago.

He had to explain Paulie's death to me, and he knew that a phone conversation wouldn't suffice. Looking reluctant but knowing there was no way around it, he timed his arrival to when I got home. He rang the bell and waited for the door to open, and finally, five minutes later, he walked in. He went around the dimly lit house and put Paulie's blanket, empty plastic bottle that was his toy, Frisbee, comb, cleanser, shampoo in a bag. They were things I couldn't bring myself to get rid of. When the dog smell on the sofa, cushions, and rug disappears, all traces of Paulie's life here will be gone.

I understood Paulie's death. My dog happened to die, and that's all there is to it. Animals want to mark their territory when they go to a new place. It's their instinct. Cats leave their scent by rubbing their faces on everything, and a badger drags his anus on the ground. A dog gets used to a place by urinating. Nobody likes an old dog that roams around a perfect house and urinates everywhere. And Se-yeon never liked dogs in the first place. Finally she pushed Paulie into the bathroom and closed the door. When Seok-ju came home he took walks with Paulie, but because of her he kept him locked in the bathroom. The dog with whom he had spent the most difficult time of his life. He tried to convince Paulie and to train him. But an old dog can't adapt to a new place. Because he already has his established ways. There were two more bathrooms downstairs, so they had no reason to open that door unless it was to take Paulie out. Leaving for Kuwait on a business trip, he pleaded with Se-yeon to walk Paulie once a day. Three days passed. She forgot about him. Paulie didn't let out a single moan, and when she finally remembered and threw open the bathroom door, he expressed his anger by flinging himself at her.

The last Sunday of April when he came to pick Paulie up, Se-yeon came with him. But she didn't look like she wanted to come into the house. We stood in the yard while he went inside to get Paulie. Se-yeon said she would try her best with him, but she wasn't confident. She adjusted her sunglasses and added, I'm sorry.

Just as she didn't want to come into the house, Paulie balked at leaving it. Se-yeon and I stood side by side for a while. I gave her some advice about Paulie. If Paulie is agitated or violent, don't ever look him in the eyes; if he comes near in a threatening way, she should stand still like a tree. With her feet together and her hands around her neck and her elbows touching her chest. The neutral stance that demonstrates to the dog that you mean no harm. So, like a tree, I said. I guess I would look a little stupid like that, Se-yeon replied, and it's possible that we nodded and smiled a little.

Paulie probably wanted to express how angry he was. A dog expresses himself like a dog. With his mouth wide open, showing his canines, he jumped toward Se-yeon's neck. Because it's a good place to lightly bite and let go. Se-yeon, in terror, instinctively slammed Paulie's head with what she had in her

147

hand—a skillet. A dog and a human have to understand each other's language, and that didn't exist between Paulie and her. Paulie's sharp, pointy teeth were about to touch her neck and she swung her arm and hit Paulie's head and Paulie dropped to the floor. A dog's teeth could rip through thick deerskin. She had to protect her life from an angry dog. Trembling with fear, she hit Paulie's head over and over again with the skillet. Even if the dog merely wants to warn, his teeth are strong enough to gouge a hole into a child's cheek. Nobody could fault her. She kept pounding and screaming until Paulie was dead, his legs stretched out, blood from the top of his head drenching his thin, soft, silky coat and the floor.

I told her, Like a tree, I said to myself.

He looked at me, wondering what I was talking about.

*Please go away now.*

I didn't want to cry or vomit in front of him. Afraid I would ask him to stay, that I would cling to him saying how difficult it was, I firmly told him again to leave.

It hurts me, too, that things turned out this way, he said, looking down as he slipped his shoes back on.

It's probably more guilt you're feeling than hurt, I said, adding, That is, if you're a human being.

I wave off Chef, who wanted to walk me home, and leave. If he comes to my door I might not be able to say goodbye. I want to cry and sit somewhere. My chest tightens. I have so many things I want to say, about to burst out of my chest. I drank too much. My feet are walking but I don't know where I'm going. I don't know where my house is. It's May but I'm shivering. If I had a glass of water, I think I could get a grip on myself. I think I'd be able to figure out how to get home. I walk unevenly into the underground walkway as if I'm being sucked in. Large empty boxes are lining either side. I steady myself, a hand on the wall, and throw up. I wipe my mouth with the back of my hand. Small, black, round grains of sand roll onto my hand. The caviar. They look like ovaries. I have to vomit again. I force myself up and look around for the exit. A man's head pops out of a box at the end of the line, like a mushroom. The homeless are lying in the lidless boxes, one in each. Yeah, because it's nighttime. Everyone is sleeping. I have to go home. I try to straighten up and walk in a straight line. The man, who has a cigarette in his mouth, spits outside his cardboard box and glares at me like a wild beast. I stop. I raise the corners of my mouth and smile. The man extinguishes the cigarette. I take a few steps toward him. He tosses the cigarette lightly near my feet, as if to test my reaction. I smile again and raise my eyebrows and widen my eyes. I briefly avert my gaze, then look straight at him again and feign another smile. This is what it's like, I realize. I tense my legs so I don't sway. This is what it was? That smile you gave him, I say to Se-yeon. The man gets up from his box and pulls my arm. Let go, I giggle. The man puts his hand over my mouth. I want to sing and drum. Like at the beginning of a festival, when a fire is set on a living sacrifice. *I won't yell, let go.* I'm tugged into the box. The men in the other boxes peek out and turn their faces away, bored, not interested. The man, breathing hard, pushes my shoulder to the bottom of the box with his knee. I grin. *Don't hurry. All you have to do is just poke me, like I'm a small fish.* The man, standing in front of me blocking my view, lowers his zipper. A short thick thing with protruding veins nods toward me, close to me, as if it would poke my eyes. Like one of the thousand taste buds on your tongue when you look through a microscope. The living bumps on the tongue, pillars that can discern what is tasty. As if I'm holding on to a lifeline, I grab it with both hands and hang on. *Hey.* I open my mouth. *What do I look like right now? Do I look like a woman? No, no, do I look like a cow or a pig about to be sacrificed? When you kill a cow you stick a knife deep into its throat. Then hot, thick blood bubbles out. And then you cut off its head. Then you take a hook and spear the tongue to keep it still.* Shit, what's she mumbling? The man, who is gripping my hair with one hand, fluidly lights a cigarette with his other hand. He exhales into my face. I swallow it. The man knows now. That I can't leave, that I don't have a reason to. Tears drop noisily onto the bottom of the box, like the hot, thick blood of a cow. *It's really so bright here, like the middle of a market, like the butcher's, where dead animals are laid out under bright lights. I want to be my own sacrifice. Before you kill me, sprinkle flour on my head. Decorate me with cornstalks. Now kill me, eat me up. Or burn me and let me fly away. The smell of me roasting will go up to the sky and make the gods happy. The people who set fire to the sacrificial should shout with glee. I will burn up. I want to die cleanly. I want to be reborn. The flames will push toward me insistently and rage with force and fall slowly calm. I want that pure feeling, the desire of first love. If not, just melt me so I become clear water, what I was in the beginning. I want to erase this pain. Here, here's my mouth. This is the entrance that shows who I am. Stuff it up, stick a blade into my throat. Shut it up. Hurry up.* Kneeling, holding the huge taste bud with both hands, I open my mouth as wide as I can. It pushes into my mouth without hesitation. But tell me, why was she holding a skillet at that moment? Why was she holding it at that moment? I ask, choking, my eyes searching the air.

# JUNE

*Every moving thing that is alive shall be food for you.*

—Genesis 9:3

# CHAPTER 24

T HE DAY I'M PROMOTED to chef de cuisine I buy a pair of
shoes with a pearl in the bottom of each sole. At work I
wear flats or sneakers, but heels are fitting for special days. These
are designed so that you would never know there was a pearl
nestled in the soles if you didn't flip the shoes over. I feel great
when I walk in them, knowing that a pearl follows my every
step. As a gift to myself, there is nothing better. I wish a day as
special as these shoes would come to me. As chef de cuisine I
have to oversee the kitchen and be responsible for almost everything that happens. Being promoted within five months of coming back to Nove is very quick, even for me. Yet the staff seems
to think I was the right choice. I might have been seen as a
threatening presence. But I never left the kitchen and my knife
was glued to my hand and I did chores people hated to do. I
came to work early and prepared all the ingredients for the stations and made sure everything was perfect. If I missed the last
train after working in the test kitchen, I napped on the cot in

Chef's office without bothering to change my clothes. I wasn't exhausted or tired. Like someone born in a kitchen, I cooked all day and I thought only about food.

The kitchen feels familiar and comfortable, more than ever before, much like a small universe rotating in an orderly way or a small house made just for me. The rattling of dishes and the *psst–psst* of steam and the crackling of food in pans and the bubbling of water: The sounds around me are like the rhythmic reverberations of a mysterious bell. The perfect order of each person working at the stove and the cutting board, chopping and frying and boiling and plating in unison, is consistent and beautiful, an intricately choreographed dance. I remember Grandmother saying that the door to the kitchen should always be open. This lively clatter seeps into the dining room from the open kitchen, filling it with a happy, musical ruckus. I especially like the busy noisiness of Friday nights, when we have the most customers. My entire being is elated as if I'm eating food with too much saffron. I see the true beauty of all ingredients. It's been thirteen years since I started cooking, but only now am I beginning to know what I'm doing. The ends of my fingers are alert, like I'm the world's best safecracker. I think I've regained balance in my life.

Once, during my cooking classes, as we made the mayonnaise for *poulet roti,* one student grumbled playfully that she didn't understand why she had to stir egg yolks at a constant speed, causing everyone to laugh. I explained why, seriously. Otherwise the molecules will become unstable and the mayonnaise will separate. There is balance in taste, too, and an unbalanced taste can't captivate the eater. In order to create harmony, you have to think about balance, and to get balance in the kitchen you have to follow seemingly insignificant but crucial rules.

The new prep cook was fired within two weeks because of his failure to follow the rules. He put garlic, which has to be chopped and sliced and minced by hand, in the food processor behind Chef's back, but was caught when Chef came into the kitchen unexpectedly in the early morning. In Italian food, garlic is as important as the indispensable tomato. We inevitably use a large amount throughout the day. To maintain the freshness and the sharp scent of garlic, you can't freeze it or chop it before it's needed. You lay the knife flat to smash cloves of garlic, never using a food processor. As soon as you put garlic in a machine, its scent disappears. Chef's rule is that people who can't be bothered to handle garlic by hand don't have the right to cook. Garlic, especially roasted, shiny, brown garlic, sweet and creamy, is one of Chef's most favored ingredients, used in almost every dish at Nove. Whirring it in the food processor behind Chef's back is worse than stealing wine or meat. Very rarely does Chef personally fire someone. But there are no exceptions if it has to do with violating the most basic rules of the kitchen. When he does fire someone, Chef is firm and cold and detached. That new cook, who was about to take out a garbage bag leaking liquid, ripped off his uniform and left the premises. He might have thought, All this over stupid garlic. But we all know Chef was right.

We decide to hire two more cooks, including a saucier. We have twenty applicants, about half of whom graduated from the American CIA—the Harvard of cooking schools—and the Italian ICIF. If educational background were the only factor considered, I wouldn't have the qualifications to become chef de cuisine. During a break on a Sunday afternoon, Chef and Manager Park and I conduct interviews. I don't want to participate but Chef insists, as if he knew we would notice different qualities and open up a good debate. Of the twenty applicants, I like A and B, Chef focuses on C and D, and Manager Park picks B and D. So Chef and I chose completely different applicants.

Patience is the most important characteristic of a cook.

Otherwise you won't be able to get through days of doing the same thing over and over again in a narrow kitchen. The kitchen staff is a small, friendly army. Sometimes it's good to be an individual, but you also have to be able to work with others. Both Chef and I believe that the head chef has to keep a clear head at all times, be meticulous and steady. All applicants submitted an Italian recipe they were most confident in making. A and B's recipes revere the simple and the basic, and C and D's are individualistic and creative. Chef says A and B are overly plain and unimaginative, and I argue that C and D ignore the basics and are show-offs. I stand my ground even though I know Chef has a good eye for these things, and Chef digs in his heels. Finally, in the spirit of compromise, we choose B and D. They won't have a hard time fitting in: Neither is the product of a formal culinary education, but both have the most experience. It's an accepted wisdom in the industry that you can teach someone to cook but you can't teach them personality. So it's not a bad choice if the cook loyal to the basics and the creative cook have gentle souls. Still, I feel defeated.

# CHAPTER 25

W HAT ARE YOU DOING this fine Sunday?"
"I don't know what to make with this," I smile em-
barrassedly.

"With what?"

"A carp."

A hearty laugh reverberates through the phone. It's been a
while since I heard Uncle laugh. Uncle can make phone calls to
the outside twice a week, on Wednesdays and Sundays. I'm off
today but I still came in to work. Because we ordered a larger than
usual shipment of perch and croaker, they threw in three carp. I
start to get nervous when people don't order seafood dishes, leaving the fridge filled with fish. Like steak, fish is expensive but
easy to cook. The simpler the dish, the better its taste. But I
need to cultivate a different recipe, something other than baking and frying and steaming.

"Try baking it stuffed with garlic and herbs."

I smile. Grandmother's recipe. I already cleaned out the innards because I was thinking in that direction. Grandmother

didn't like the sourness of lemon, but it should be added to minimize the fishy taste and accentuate the fresh scent. "Do you think so? Or do you think I should pan-fry it in olive oil and plate it with artichokes?"

"That sounds good, too." To make me laugh, Uncle loudly smacks his lips into the receiver.

This is not the time to tell him about Paulie. Uncle asks me if I could come visit next week. Visiting days are Fridays, but that's when the kitchen is at its busiest. I tell him I can. I feel uneasy leaving the kitchen, but this is the first time Uncle has asked me to come visit him.

"Is something going on, Uncle?"

"Will you bring me a washcloth?"

I'm surprised.

There are certain things you can't bring to the hospital. Obviously disposable razors or knives, scissors, nail clippers, clothes hangers, lighters, matches—and also things like blankets or long ties or belts. Even rice cakes aren't allowed, because you can choke on them.

"No, it's not what you think. I don't feel clean when I shower. They don't have those here." Uncle laughs.

Glad that Uncle knows what I'm thinking, I place the carp on the chopping block. I only hear Uncle's voice but I think I understand. I think he really just needs the washcloth. "But I don't think that's possible yet, Uncle," I tell him, laughing, and hang up.

If someone close to you is an alcoholic, you can't sympathize with him. Instead you need to practice restricting your own confused feelings, understanding that you feel the way you do because you're near an alcoholic. And you can't ever try to deal with an alcoholic by yourself. I wasn't able to do anything for Uncle, but he was gradually trying to get better. And the family-therapy sessions gave both of us new hope. Alcoholics' families often deny that an alcoholic is among them and unconsciously try to keep the patient in a codependent state, in an ongoing alcoholic haze. So the family is sometimes the victim or the onlooker or even the wrongdoer. The therapy sessions allowed us to understand each other's positions. But hearing the word *codependency* was like stepping on a nail. The important thing is that Uncle is starting to change—a change different from the transformation I've undergone.

Uncle, who had been passive toward the treatment program, now plays badminton and Ping-Pong with the other patients and joins calligraphy and origami sessions. I wonder if Uncle is adapting to his environment so he can remain in the hospital, instead of completing his treatment. Once, I asked him in a suggestive tone, Don't you want a drink? As if I would have given one to him if he had wanted. Uncle, lost in thought for a while, shook his head. *Of course I want to sometimes, but if I have the urge to drink I have a conversation with myself.* How, I asked. *I ask myself, What would happen if I don't quit now?* I nodded earnestly. There are three levels in the treatment process— detox, rehabilitation, and social adaptation—and Uncle seems to have arrived at the second level. But why does that make me feel unsettled and empty?

If I could talk to Uncle's wife one last time, I would ask her if she really loved him. I don't understand why she killed herself but I think I could cook for her now. I pour an inch of olive oil into the hot pan to fry the red carp. For the sauce I mix together white wine and fish stock. When I make something for the first time, I get tense but I don't falter or hesitate. I sweep sliced artichokes into the same pan to crisp them. I season them with salt and pepper. I plate the carp and garnish it with the artichokes. I drizzle the sauce over it.

No. Something is missing. When you make a dish for the

first time, it's important to have a feel for it. I stare at the carp and nod. I find a jar filled with nuts and take out some almonds. With the side of my knife, I tap the almonds to peel them and slice them in slivers, as if they are garlic. I place the white almonds around the carp's eye. I pick up the eyeball that I took out before putting the carp in the pan and nestle it back into its place. Food lovers don't even glance at a fish dish if its eyes are missing. The almond garnish spotlights the white of the carp's eye. It's bright and clear, fitting for a dish made for a dead person. Try it, Aunt, I say, my voice faltering. Many creative, imaginative women suffer from anorexia. If I had been closer to her I might have been able to help her over time, as I did with Munju. But she chose a more dramatic method, an ending fitting for a creative and imaginative woman. I look down at the dish. The fish's eye is fresh and alien-like, asking me, How can you see anything, the way you're stumbling around in the dark?

# CHAPTER 26

I'VE RECEIVED OFFERS to write a cookbook several times, both from Mun-ju's magazine and from other publishers. I would have enough for a book if I compiled all the recipes I've published in women's magazines and food publications. I refused every time for two reasons: I believed that there was no such thing as a unique recipe, and even Chef hadn't written a cookbook. If I had a chicken I would be able to make a hundred dishes with it. To highlight only one way to cook a chicken would be ignoring the possibilities. You have to be able to cook a chicken according to your mood and intuition, and the side dishes and the ingredients to be stuffed into the chicken have to change with the seasons. Anyone could write a book about a basic chicken recipe, and that book probably exists anyway. But more importantly, Chef is the one who developed my palate and helped me grow beyond it. It would make me uneasy if I were to write a cookbook before he did—it wouldn't be ethical. I might have thought differently if I still had my cooking classes. It would have been a way to promote the classes and K as a chef, and at the time I wasn't thinking of Chef unless I was using his methods for a recipe in a magazine or in class as if I'd come up with them on my own.

Anyway, now I don't have time to think about a cookbook: It's more practical and invigorating to think of a different chicken recipe. Chef, on the other hand, is considering that very idea. Before dinner service, he calls me to the office and asks if I could help him write a cookbook. Even someone you think you know well can make you flustered. It's as if he secretly told me a broken tree branch will come back to life if I blow on it. I don't believe this and neither does he, but the sad thing is that I consider his proposition for a moment, even as he watches me with pitying eyes. Now I feel more than flustered. I feel deflated. Could it be that all he wants to do is write a book on food? I'm not being creative or open-minded. It's not a good attitude to have when I'm cooking. I ask, frowning, Why so suddenly?

Years ago, Chef told me that Apicius is always mentioned in books about the origins of cooking. He was a first-century Roman chef who wrote the oldest surviving cookbook, *On the Subject of Cooking,* and was the first cook to really incorporate eggs in dishes. At the time, Romans were fighting ennui. Epicureanism was in vogue, and the eater and the cook desired to break boundaries by creating dishes with pig's nipples and genitalia or stuffed winter rats. Cooks had to satisfy the finicky tastes of their patrons, patrons who were ready to eat anything different. Apicius worked to create an ingenious dish that had never existed before. Finally, after completing his book, he killed himself. He exhausted everything he had, just like an artist. Afterward, other cooks named Apicius appeared and similar cookbooks were published. I still remember vowing, as I chopped leeks in skills class, that I wouldn't be one of the later Apiciuses. People change. Everything changes. There's nothing remarkable about Chef changing. We've never spoken about it but we've been supportive and nonjudgmental of each other. But I don't want to do this. Anyone else can do it; it doesn't have to be me.

Chef plays with a crystal water glass sitting on the desk, his face expressionless. I watch his large, darkened left hand holding the glass. A hand that has been broken and sewn and cut. The hand I've been looking up to since I was twenty, the hand that moved efficiently and effectively in the kitchen. Chef picks up a teaspoon and stirs the water in the glass. Even water moves if you stir it, he says. When I stop, the water's going to continue swirling like a little hurricane for a while. I mean, what would happen if everything stopped? He swallows hard. I wonder if it's hard for him to vocalize a simple thought, just as it's hard to make a simple dish. *You know the foods that make you feel better when you eat them? The kind of food that gives you pure joy? I want to make a list of happiness.* Chef stops talking. As if to say, I'm doing this, whether you help me or not. I stay there a little longer, then leave the office and go up the stairs.

A list of happiness.

Is that even possible? I look out the picture window as people come into Nove, study the menu, look toward the kitchen in anticipation of the food, stare into each other's eyes across a vase with a single violet in it. Nobody is silent in a restaurant. Everyone is smiling or talking or eating. Maybe the table was the birthplace of language. A repetitive gathering place for meals and routine activities is conducive to talking, to conversations. Food goes into a mouth and words come out of it, just like a door. Talking and tasting, expressions of desire, happen in the mouth, on the tongue, and the mouth is the entrance to our bodies, revealing who we are.

The restaurant is filled with upbeat, happy chatter. Red lips, swollen in expectation of warm food and words, float, cloudlike. People move closer, whispering secrets and eating and feeding one another food. When you whisper and eat, the tip of your tongue, glistening with saliva, peeks out, sparkling like a red jewel. If you touch the roof of your mouth with your tongue and sing, *lalalala*, your bones vibrate with the sound. This gleeful clamor erupts when you eat something delicious.

Now I remember the cookbook I wanted to write—food that brings positive change, the vivid sensations and tastes and textures of my youth, the scents of memories and the stories behind them. Once I wanted to write a book similar to Chef's. Back then, I whispered and talked and ate and drank and laughed like all the others. I sat close to friends in small circles, like winter bees trying to survive the cold. Am I certain we loved each other? Happiness comes through the mouth, but the mouth is also the doorway through which it walks out. If you lock the door to your body from the inside, the inner darkness traps you. If you're the kind of person who doesn't keep promises, the mouth is merely a dark, lightless cave.

# CHAPTER 27

I OPEN MY FRONT DOOR and Mun-ju pokes her head out from behind the pocket door. I pause, taken by surprise. It's been a long time since someone greeted me when I got home. In January, when I was in bed for ten days, Mun-ju wrote down the contact information for the hospital Uncle was in and made a copy of my keys, saying, So this won't happen again. I'm not bedridden anymore but something in me is shattered. Even if something disappears it isn't completely gone. After Paulie's death I've become more attuned to sound. I'm not scared by big noises, like the sound of thunder or lightning or fireworks. But the sound of rain coasting down the windows, the door closing, the fridge whirring, a few grains of rice falling to the floor, my own breathing—I feel those more immediately than the pounding of a drum. And the sounds I hear—Paulie's slow footsteps, his sniffing, his breathing. One night, when Paulie's death finally sank in, his sounds wounding me, I had to stifle my moans. Paulie used to give a single bark when the wind rustled the leaves, when he sauntered into the yard, when I brushed my teeth, when the blender was whirring, when I was grinding coffee beans. I keep brushing my teeth even after they're clean, in the darkness, to feel Paulie coming up to me and pressing his wet nose on the back of my knees. *Yeah, I remember. We shared something deep, something fundamental. Right, Paulie?*

Now I run alone on the track at night.

Everything in this world, including those long dead, makes noise. But I can't tell even Mun-ju that Paulie runs next to me, his teeth suppressing his panting.

"Exercise is fine and good, but not right before you sleep."

"It was always at this time."

"What?"

I stay quiet.

"Oh, right. That's true." Mun-ju nods.

I get up and boil water and steep some lavender. We sit on the sofa, side by side. Mun-ju has just returned from a week in Venegono Superiore, a small town about an hour from Milan, for a special feature about slow food. If you take the train from there and travel south for two hours, you arrive in Tuscany. The last time I went to Italy through Nove's program, I learned how to butcher pigs and cattle, observing butchers for three weeks. It was a unique chance, but when the most renowned butcher in the region pulled out the backbone of a pig lying on its side, with a flourish, I let out a surprised shriek, so I lost the opportunity to learn more. The butcher's glare was cold and jagged, reproachful. The way Chef looked at me if I made a mistake at the chopping block as a novice.

"Are you already done with the article?"

"The issue's already out. But it's not that interesting."

"What isn't?"

"This slow-food movement."

"Didn't it come from the desire to live at a slower pace?"

"Yeah. You ride a bike instead of driving a car, you take naps

166

in the afternoon, and you cook the fruit and vegetables from your garden."

"What's wrong with that?"

"You have too much time to think."

"You don't like that?"

"A happy person doesn't have that much to think about."

We laugh. A bitter laugh, as if to acknowledge that we are far from being happy.

"How are things?" Mun-ju asks.

"Fine, I guess."

"I stopped by Nove yesterday afternoon for a cup of tea but you weren't there. Where were you?"

Yesterday afternoon I met Mr. Choe at the Shilla Hotel café. "He asked if I wanted to move to a different kitchen."

Mun-ju doesn't know what I'm talking about.

"He's going to open a restaurant."

"Chef is opening another one?"

"No, Mr. Choe."

"Mr. Choe from Mido?"

"Yeah."

"So is he scouting you?"

I don't answer. Was that what he meant? Mr. Choe said that he was going to renovate a two-story wine bar into an Italian restaurant. The location is great and so is the salary he mentioned, much more than what I make at Nove. He said that I would be sent overseas to learn about food for one month every year. Every cook who starts the day peeling hundreds of potatoes wants this, and, unless your dream is to run your own restaurant, this is the best—and rarest—opportunity. I smiled at Mr. Choe. He said, We should keep this quiet from Chef for the time being. He wetted his lips and added, When you get to my age, you start wanting a cook. Your own cook.

A chef prefers customers that keep him on his toes. You

ignore the customer who orders steak well-done or the person who asks for chicken. People who don't know what they're eating order chicken at Italian restaurants. Those who eat well-done steak don't appreciate the taste of meat. Gourmets want something that's not on the menu. They eat only plump Cornish hens or castrated roosters or the choice parts of a whole roasted duck. They want swan, as if it's the eighteenth century. They understand that taste is triggered by the sense of touch, through the lips, and they want to have a mouth longer than the beak of a crane, to enjoy the ecstasy of food sliding down to their intestines. Cesare Ripa's *Crapula* satirizes the fat stomachs and crane necks of extreme pleasure seekers. Food lovers ignore even death threats when it comes to something they want to eat. The possibility of death is why gourmets love blowfish. If you put a thin piece of blowfish—sliced so thin that the cook's fingerprint is visible—in your mouth, your lips redden and heat up and tremble from the fear and excitement of death. Your spirits rise and saliva pools in your mouth. Finally a childlike smile spreads across your face.

The obsession over food is tenacious. The eighteenth-century writer Nicholas-Thomas Barthe, who wrote *Les Fausses Infidélités*, had the habit of eating everything on the table. Barthe did not have good eyesight and was fearful that he wouldn't be able to see all the food and might miss some of it. He would hound his servants, asking, Have I eaten this? Have I eaten that? He died from indigestion. King Darius, who liked beef, put up curtains to hide from the others as he ate an entire cow. Balzac, a coffee addict, drank forty to fifty cups a day and died of gastritis. The philosopher Democritus, upon realizing that his life was coming to an end, deprived himself each day of one food until there was only a jar of honey left. He stuck his nose in the jar and smelled the honey, and as soon as the jar was taken away, he died, at the age of 109.

President Mitterand had the most extreme obsession with ortolan, a bird on the verge of extinction and illegal to eat. In 1995, knowing he didn't have much time left before he died of cancer, Mitterand invited friends to a New Year's Eve dinner. The main course was ortolan. This bird, which signifies purity and the love of Jesus, was considered the best dish in the world, and after it's roasted in the oven you put the entire thing in your mouth, on your tongue, when it's still very hot. You enjoy the feeling of the fat spilling down your throat, and as it cools, you start crunching on the bird's head and the crunch rings in your ears rhythmically. That night, Mitterand broke the tradition of eating only one bird per person and ate two. The next day he couldn't keep anything down and soon passed away—ortolan became his last supper.

The worst kind of gourmet is the one who tries to fulfill his perverse sexual desires with food. Such people do not truly love food. True gourmets understand that the mingling of curiosity and fear produces a heightened joy. They try to taste the new and revere beauty and deliciousness. Great chefs exist behind such gourmets.

"So what did you tell him?"

"That I'd just stay at Nove."

"Why?"

"Because I don't want anything more."

"That's an odd way to say it. Just say you like Nove."

"Yeah, I want to stay there."

"Yeah."

"Do you think that was the right thing to do?" I ask.

"I do."

"You know, to Chef."

"Don't worry, I won't say anything."

"I think that would be best."

"The rainy season has been going on for so long."

"It'll be over soon."

"After the peak season, how about we go somewhere for a few days?"

". . . Sure."

"Where should we go?" Mun-ju goes into the bathroom, yawning. From my dresser, I take out a cotton T-shirt and pajama pants for Mun-ju and place them on the table. I pick up the heavy bag she'd flung onto the floor. The July edition of *Wine & Food* is sticking out. *She said it was about Italy.* I flip through the pages. The days when I worked from morning to night for eleven months at Nove and then took the last month off to wander through Italy eating and learning feels like a dream. My hand pauses from flipping the pages. I turn a few back.

A familiar face.

People I know.

I hear water running in the bathroom.

On the "Special Interview" page, a man and a woman sit on a long U-shaped butcher block, wearing matching white shirts and jeans and bright smiles. Their arms are around each other's shoulders and their feet may be swinging.

I know them. I can't really read the title.

I think it says *Lee Se-yeon's new cooking class* and maybe also *a modern kitchen built by the young architect Han Seok-ju.* The magazine is snatched out of my hands.

*Mun-ju, what is this?* I ask silently. Mun-ju's eyes waver uncertainly like someone caught trying to hide something, welling with tears. *No, no.* I shake my head. *Don't cry, just tell me. Tell me the truth. I don't want to be the last to know. Tell me, Mun-ju.*

Silence doesn't flow, it spreads. Like the rings in a pond when you throw a rock, it gets bigger and bigger and finally ripples throughout all of space. And it skims the body like a spasm.

# CHAPTER 28

I T'S NOT EMBARRASSING to be injured in the kitchen, but cutting your finger is not a good way to start your morning. I slit the first section of my pinky as I cut up a chicken. I don't even remember sharpening the knife. I brush over the blade. It's dull. In a chaotic kitchen where many people have to work together, bumping into each other, you have to keep your knife a little dull, unlike in your home kitchen. If the knife is too sharp you can seriously injure yourself if you don't pay attention for a split second. You don't really need a sharp knife unless you have to handle poultry or do delicate work with vegetables. I'm embarrassed, not that I cut my hand in the kitchen in front of everyone, but that I was hurt by such a dull blade.

You work with fire and knives in the kitchen, where small and large dangers lurk. The ideal place to hide a destructive instinct. I'm engulfed by this unstable urge as I watch red blood dripping onto the cutting board, feeling joy as if a frustration has disappeared. Or relief that this has stopped a bigger calamity. If there's no possibility of danger, I might not feel tense when I hold a knife.

Instead of bandaging my finger, I put it in my mouth. A metallic tang spreads in my mouth as if I licked steel. Maybe I should keep my knife sharper so I would use it more carefully and thoughtfully. I start grinding it on the sharpening stone in the corner of the table. When I'm very busy and I don't have time to hone the knife, I just rub it against a sharpening steel a few times. But it's always best to use a sharpening stone. Although it's quicker to use the sharpening steel, the blade goes bad quickly.

My workstation has stainless-steel containers holding salt and whole pepper and pasta sauce and olive oil and various herbs and chopped parsley and red and white wines and diced tomato and butter and brandy, along with long chopsticks and ladles and tongs and large spoons and pans and pots. Typical items for a workstation. But the knife is indispensable. If you have to get one thing as a cook, it must be a good chef's knife. A good knife is more important than your passion for cooking. If you have a good knife in your hand, you have an automatic desire to cook. Every cook has at least one knife that is his own. For a Western cook, a knife is his third arm, as is a ladle for a Chinese chef. In truth, knife skills get the cook noticed.

I have three knives. A thin, long, Japanese sushi knife for fish and a short and flexible knife for chicken or duck. And a plain German Henkel that I use for all other purposes. But usually the Henkel is good enough. When I'm trimming vegetables I use the tip of the knife, and when I'm handling something bigger or firmer I use its end. It's very old and chipped but I haven't parted with it. When I started at Nove, I took up this knife, which had been collecting dust in its case in Grandmother's kitchen. Grandmother had several knives, including a serrated one for slicing bread or fruit. It was my favorite when I was younger, but after I started to cook I couldn't find it. Chef's knife is a Japanese Global—it has a slightly pointy tip but is still a plain kitchen knife. The knife stand is crowded with all of our knives, sticking out at 45-degree angles. Each cook can find his knife in an instant, even if the handles are virtually identical. It's important to have a knife that feels right.

I sense Manager Park and the new saucier exchanging looks of *What's going on with her?* I stand at my station, gripping the knife as if someone might snatch it out of my hand, blood still seeping from my finger. I catch him placing a gentle hand on her waist when they pass by. People say it's impossible to hide poverty and illness and love, but the gaze of staff members when they fall in love is the hardest to hide in the crowded narrow kitchen. Everyone finds out even if it's only been for a day—they're in a clear glass fishbowl. There's no place as easy to fall in love as a kitchen. But if they break up, one person always ends up quitting, usually the woman. Separation is common, but it's not altogether rare to hear of couples who marry or open a restaurant together.

What was love to me? I put my knife down on the chopping block. To me, love was like music—I could feel it and both my head and heart reacted to it even though it wasn't taught to me. Love was like food—I salivated, it whetted my appetite. Love was music and food. Every pore felt a pure elation, I lamented but was uplifted, I was confused but desirous. It began as a simple thing but it was beautiful and sensual and affected my whole being. I used to think this described love.

More than three pages of Se-yeon and Seok-ju's pictures were featured in the magazine. In one picture they faced each other playfully in her soon-to-be-opened cooking-class kitchen, hands dripping with honey. Licking honey from each other's palms to signify that they would share food and loving words was a Germanic tradition of promising love. This would have been

173

Mun-ju's idea. Although she didn't want to, once she decided to interview them the editor in her would have done her best to get a good picture, an original one. Most don't know the legend of honey. Mun-ju is the one who told me this story. Thankfully there wasn't a picture of them licking each other's palms. Mystics slicked honey on their hands and tongues to fight evil and realize good. I should be the one with honeyed palms now, not them.

*Be careful. Love is like a mushroom—when you harvest mushrooms you shouldn't pull them out of the ground but carefully cut them with a small knife. So they will keep growing.* I want to say this to Manager Park and the saucier. But for me, love is no longer music or food or honey or mushrooms. Everything has changed now.

I hear something. Blood coursing, bones breaking, blood stopping. Cooks are knife-wielding artists. We express ourselves with our hands. The kitchen could easily become a scene of carnage. With my knife, I fearlessly pin the plump cock's comb to the cutting board, the cock's comb that glistens proud and red, like the arrogant tongue of a liar.

# CHAPTER 29

LOVE AND HUNGER ARE ONE, just like the seed and germ of fruit. Physical symptoms that propel your life. Love and hunger, the most instinctive reflexes, are regulated by the same part of the brain. If neither is satisfied, you are overwhelmed with rage. There aren't very many things you can do to get beyond rage other than to continue eating. Me yelling, me sobbing, me holding a bag of chips all day. A simple montage of me six months ago. When I chewed on thin, crispy chips, shrieks and bone-breaking crunches and sounds of strangling rang loudly in my ears, pounding against my eardrums. A chip is designed so that it's impossible to put the entire thing in your mouth. The wider you open your mouth to stuff in the chip, the more it affects your eardrums, delivering the irritating chewing sound directly into your ear. I became addicted to chips because of the sheer joy of it—like a kid tasting the fizz of his first carbonated drink. As I lay on the couch for days and the chewing noise grew louder and louder, my inner instinct of attack grew stronger and stronger. I felt unease that I wouldn't be able to control myself.

I wasn't going to retrieve this love with rage. I put down the bag of chips and pressed my lips together. I couldn't hear a thing. I got off the sofa slowly, in resignation. It was just an illusion that I'd never expressed anger. I'd revealed all of my emotions to him as he moved like a shadow through the house. I wish it hadn't reached a point where he couldn't bear it anymore. Now I regret it. I think that was when I developed a fear of opening my mouth. It's hard to eat with someone I'm not close to. When I taste food in the kitchen I turn around, dip my finger in it, stick it into my mouth, and close my lips around it. But when I see round objects that look hard on the outside but are soft inside, like button mushrooms or an eggplant, I have the urge to chew and lick them. Is it a symptom of my unfulfilled sexuality? Or a gourmet's curiosity? Once I had to clap my hand over my mouth when I was making an Asian-inspired salad dressing of mayonnaise, soy sauce, minced garlic, and sesame oil. Neither white nor yellow, half transparent, fairly thick. I recalled the man who'd stood upright and aimed directly into my mouth. It was like swallowing a mouthful of stew without thinking. Hot and sour and slightly bitter. I wonder what it would be like if I were to try it again—a common feeling after a first experience. When it was aimed at my mouth, I was surprised that I was able to open my mouth that wide, that I could be that instantly and quickly elated, that it was such a familiar taste. Who was making lip-smacking noises? Was it he who was holding on to my head, or me, lying on the bottom of the box as if in supplication? I tossed away the now-empty tube of mayonnaise. If I had an organ that I could pull out whenever I wanted and aim at someone, I think I would stand straight and stick it resolutely into someone's mouth.

If he comes back it might be a while until we have sex, like when we first met. But I don't think he will come back. Because he's finally built a new house, the house he's wanted to build, the house he dreamed of and designed with me.

Four years ago when we looked at spaces for Won's Kitchen, he was disappointed that he couldn't design and build the building. He would draw, erase, and redraw a squat, small building in red brick, the cooking class on the first floor, his office on the second, and our bedroom occupying the third. Pointing at the blueprint, I playfully said the third floor was too far from the first, where I would be spending all of my days. *Then we can put in a long pole.* He drew a long line down the middle of the drawing. I laughed, saying, I thought those things were only in fire stations where every second counts. *If you use this it'll only take a few seconds. I always wanted something like this for my own house.* He smiled brightly, earnestly, as if he would really install a fire pole if he were to build a house. I imagined him sliding down the pole from the third floor. Food would never get cold and I would never be waiting for him. I nodded shyly and pushed my hot palms into his hair. We whispered to each other, Will that day really come? Of course it will.

I still feel his hot breath near my ear, but he's already built the house. He really did put in a pole, and under the picture of him sliding down, all smiles, a caption reads, "Every second we're apart is unbearable." And a close-up of Se-yeon sitting on the sofa, her long legs crossed, gazing at him proudly. He looks different in the picture. He looks like a small brown baby monkey falling from a tree, I mumble unemotionally. And now in that house lives another woman. Not me. She's opening a cooking class. The woman who couldn't differentiate between parsley and mugwort last fall. The U-shaped open kitchen is identical to mine, and even the counters look as though they're made of the five-meter-wide marble that we chose after serious discussion. It would have been difficult to build a better kitchen. So it would have made sense to make it exactly the same. I nod slowly. The former model's cooking class in a kitchen designed by her architect boyfriend would be the talk of the town for a while. If Mun-ju's right, they're also starring in S Company's new refrigerator print-ad campaign featuring various celebrities. It's not the most fabulous comeback for a top model who had to leave the industry because of a damaged tendon near her ankle, but people will talk about it. Se-yeon looks vivacious and beautiful. *This is what people in love look like.* I feel saliva gathering in my mouth, like when I see an unfamiliar dish that tempts the eyes and the nose.

I thought love was like an olive tree, standing strong against winds and bearing green fruit as soon as the roots took hold. I'm sad, not because I can't tell him I love him but because love is no longer an olive tree or music or delicious food. But there are things that do not change. There is the kind of love that can't be redirected. Yeah, I mumble, though it's more like a moan. It's unbelievable that all of this has happened in half a year. I think it's time for me to do what I need to do. As I slowly walk into an underpass, I wonder if the skillet I gave her is in her kitchen. The skillet was one of my cherished items, with its thick bottom of three-ply stainless steel that delivers heat quickly and evenly, ideal for searing or pan-frying a thick piece of fish. Se-yeon said she wanted one, so I gave her that Italian Lagostina skillet last fall. No, she probably doesn't have it anymore. It's the skillet she used to hit Paulie. I think it's time to fetch the ball. *Isn't that right, Paulie?*

I go into a bookstore and buy a book about dissection.

# JULY

*A true gourmand is as insensible to suffering
as is a conqueror.*

—Jean-Anthelme Brillat-Savarin,
*The Physiology of Taste*

# CHAPTER 30

S UMMER BEGINS as we devein shrimp. Some cookbooks instruct you to take out the bitter, black, stringy intestine that stretches down the shrimp's back before cooking, but that's not always right. You taste bitterness first, which is stronger when hot. It is better to take out the intestine, but cooks who understand shrimp take it out only in warmer months. We're getting a lot of orders for the green pasta with shrimp and scallops—I came up with that recipe in February. At one end of the kitchen, Kwon, the prep cook, is humming, deveining shrimp with a toothpick. Meanwhile, sous chef Kim sifts flour to bake herb bread. In the morning the kitchen bristles with energy and life. Like cogs in a machine, we move about fluidly in the small space of rules and order.

Every cook is attracted to a particular ingredient. Some enjoy working with duck and turkey and others prefer beef and pork, while there are cooks who like scallops and clams or asparagus and cauliflower or potato and radish. Chef likes root vegetables and flat fish—turbot, flounder, croaker. These days he's fascinated by tea. Tea grown in the shade of tall trees in high altitude has the best flavor. During Chinese empires, virgins fourteen years and younger picked damp, soft tea leaves, wearing brand-new clothes and gloves. It's never occurred to me to use tea as an ingredient and I never thought it possible, but if Chef takes an interest in something there's no telling what will emerge. But I'm doubtful about the idea of cooking with tea. I'm not sure if it's about tea as an ingredient or because I wonder if Chef is trying to suppress his desires as he reaches a certain age.

I wish I could top Chef with my innovations. I want him to tell me, You can't make a complete dish with tea. At times I'm not sure what I want. But I know for certain that there is one thing I want. That's enough.

At one time I liked cooking with fish and roots and asparagus, like Chef, and enjoyed making dough and hand-cut pasta and bread, like sous chef Kim. I liked feeling the tips of my fingers grow gentle, not unlike playing with dark, lustrous soil. When I make dough I take a bit off and push and stretch and pull with my fingertips and make consonants like *b, c, d,* or vowels like *a, e, o, u,* and spread them across my board to make words. The way Grandmother taught Uncle and me how to read. The letters went into boiling broth at the end. Mushy vowels and consonants floated in Grandmother's bowls of noodles, and Uncle and I ate those first, vying to be the one to find more. Even after I learned to read I thought all words could be eaten.

These days I am drawn to meat. I pushed aside poultry. I need something bigger and alive and juicy and firm and animalistic, something I can't handle with one hand. Sometimes cooking is a physical battle. At times blood overflows in a banquet. To be as close to pork and beef, I take on practically all the tasks of the grill station, the way I used to when I first learned how to butcher and handle meat. On days when that's not enough, I stay in the test kitchen until dawn, roasting and frying and sauteeing and steaming and boiling and broiling. I can feel the volume and heft of the meat by sniffing the smoke filling the small kitchen. Every cook prefers a different ingredient but everyone agrees: Everything must be fresh.

I double our meat order and also order tongue. Very few people order the once-trendy steak of ox tongue anymore, so I don't stock it as often. But when a good item comes in I boil it and top it with lemon sauce and send a few slices out to the regulars, on the house. Ox tongue is so tough and chewy that you have to boil it before doing anything with it. Boiling also shrinks it to half its size. The first day the supplier brought ox tongue, I opened the box on the spot. The red tongue, frozen solid on ice, was covered in a white membrane as fresh as a juicy oyster. It was big and sensual and it looked like a part of the shoulder. It was fresher than I thought it would be but I shook my head firmly and rejected it. Suppliers always bring something good on the first order. But you can't show you're pleased with it. Then, without fail, they bring something even better the next time. To obtain an even fresher, better ingredient, you need wisdom and a little bit of cunning. It's like hunting a strong and rare animal. The next time, the supplier brought the best tongue, dripping with blood, just a day after it was slaughtered.

July is a rare red steak that melts like velvet in your mouth, with a side of green asparagus. Both the heat and the color red are sensual. And if you pair it with Tignanello, the powerful jolt of a Tuscan red, it would be a great summer-evening meal. Simple dishes made with fresh ingredients, like steak, are perfect for summer, even though it's the hardest season to handle meat properly. But a good cook has to be able to put out a delicious dish made of anything, regardless of the season. To be a good cook, you can't be afraid of challenge and failure.

I finally complete a new recipe on the first Monday of July.

An ox tongue dish. To remove the white membrane and tendons and the muscle that attaches it to the throat, I take a small, sharp knife and move it precisely in short strokes and cut out the crimson middle. The more I use my knife, the more it comes alive. My hand becomes the knife, the knife disappearing into my hand, moving freely—this is especially true when I'm holding a piece of meat in my hands. It's completely different from holding dough or handling delicate vegetables. It's as if I'm gripping onto a playful but ferocious dolphin and shoving a knife into its body.

In Japan, they believe that drinking tea is a symbol of harmony and balance, like the five fingers on your hand. So five people participate in a tea ceremony. But Chef always drinks tea alone. I take a cup and go to his table and pull up a chair. He reaches out and pours me a cup. What is this tea? It's yellow and light green and smells of arid dirt. I put my recipe on the table. He looks over the recipe silently and asks, Are you really going to use ox tongue? Skeptically. He can't understand why it's tongue, not rib eye or sirloin. If Chef makes a face like that from seeing a recipe, I have to start fresh. He puts it down and tells me my sauce of truffle oil, chopped garlic and onion, thyme, and arugula won't mask the smell of the meat. The smell of tongue doesn't disappear completely even after boiling it for six hours with vegetables and strong herbs. The sauce does have to be stronger, but I don't want to mask the tongue's true taste. I may have to think more about the sauce. Chef suggests I use watercress instead of arugula. Why didn't I think of that? I pick up my recipe and give Chef a polite nod.

# CHAPTER 31

*A*RE YOU AWAKE, *Se-yeon?*
    *I'm sure your head hurts a little but it'll get better. I didn't put that much clove in it, but it's pretty strong, right? It's an anesthetic but since it's also a spice it shouldn't be harmful. It's not like precious nutmeg, which can become poisonous. Spices are usually added at the very end but it can be dangerous depending on how they're used so you have to do it carefully. You should know this because you're going to teach cooking classes. If you have any other questions, just ask me. I'll tell you everything I know. Se-yeon, it's been a while. Was it April when you came to pick up Paulie? It's the first time since we stood in my yard that day, right? Why were you so surprised when you saw me at Costco today? I was so happy to see you.*

    *Do you still like my kitchen?*

    *I used to cook and read and drink tea and sit here and gaze out the window. And down a glass of cognac under candlelight with him and play with Paulie and listen to music. That feels like it was a really long time ago. It's only been seven months. A lot of things happened to us. What do you think? You agree with me, right? But I didn't know I would consider leaving. It's true that you can't always live the way you want to. But I guess that's not the case for you, Se-yeon.*

*I'm going to cook in this kitchen just two more times. Once for him. And once for you. Tell me what you like. I'll make it for you. Do you want to eat something in particular? Why are you sweating so much? Do you want some water? If you promise you won't yell, I'll take the towel out of your mouth.*

*The water's refreshing, isn't it? Okay, Se-yeon. If you agree with what I'm saying, just nod like that. I'm going to gag you again. Oh, don't say anything. Don't say you don't want to. Don't ask me to do things that I can't do for you. I'll let you drink as much water as you want. Are the knots too tight? But I can't untie your hands. I don't want you to get hurt. Let's just sit here together for a bit. And listen to what I have to say. I have a lot to say to you. I'm going to leave soon so I want to say everything I didn't say. You're really pretty even when you're gagged. Your skin, too, it looks so healthy and young! It makes me want to lick it, like it's chocolate. I think being beautiful is a good thing for yourself and also for people around you. Because they feel better when they're just looking at you. It's like looking at a delicious dish. How old are you again? Twenty-five? Twenty-six? Oh, twenty-seven! It's a great age. Very few women in the world have everything they want at that age. You're so lucky.*

*Tell me if there's anything you want to eat.*

*Fruit? Vegetables? Or fish? You should be able to answer such a simple question. I guess you wouldn't want any meat? Okay, I know. Why would I forget that you're practically a vegetarian? Of course, this isn't about you, but vegetarians are annoying. There are so many things to eat in the world and they give up that opportunity, voluntarily. Vegetarians make it impossible for a cook to do her best work. No, I know. I know that you're not one of those people. But a person who cooks can't have prejudices against food or be afraid of eating*

*like you are. Not eating is basically a refusal of everything, includ-*
*ing sex. And you're already so thin and you like sleeping with him,*
*isn't that right? What's taking you so long, I said I would make*
*whatever you want. Is it because there are too many things you*
*want to eat?*

*Everyone likes different food. Did you know that Hemingway*
*loved oysters? I think I mentioned it in class once. Kant liked to*
*slather mustard on everything he ate, so he always had a bottle with*
*him. Heraclitus liked greens and vegetables, like you, but he was*
*lonely and quick-tempered. Plato liked olives and dried figs and Hei-*
*degger enjoyed potato salad and Diogenes loved wine and Toulouse-*
*Lautrec liked drinking port sprinkled with nutmeg and Cleopatra*
*was partial to the hoof of a baby camel. Just imagine the ecstasy they*
*would have experienced after eating their favorite foods. Don't you*
*think it would have been beautiful to witness? You know how to*
*make that expression, too, right? I want to see it again. You were re-*
*ally beautiful then. When you were lying together, your thighs on top*
*of each other. Oh, sorry. I happened to catch you back then. That was*
*the most erotic sex I've ever seen. Because you were both so immersed*
*in it. I almost fell in love with you then. When your tongues were in*
*each other's mouths it looked like you were breathing, singing into*
*each other. That amazing feeling, I felt it too. Sex is good, no? Every*
*food is the result of a sexual act of an animal or plant.*

*You see that basket of fruit on the table? Once I was going to eat*
*an apple but there was this black-bean-like fleck on it. On the surface*
*of the red Jonathan apple. I rubbed it with my finger and it hap-*
*pened to be a piece of black nail polish. This is a little while after you*
*came to my cooking class. Remember? You were the only person who*
*came to learn how to cook with nail polish on. And black, at that. That*
*week we didn't even have class. Se-yeon, did you come here often when*
*I wasn't here? Did you sit here with him and eat fruit while I wasn't*
*home? Even so, you shouldn't have left behind that fleck of nail pol-*
*ish. Black stands out. Se-yeon, you look like perfect pottery but you*

*have an unexpected carelessness to you. No, I guess it could be all my fault. No matter how tasty and useful a potato is, when it starts to sprout you have to cut it out.*

*Still not hungry? Then should we make something simple? What about caviar on toast? I wanted to make something special for you. I still have so much to say; it's a waste to be in the kitchen by myself. But this caviar is excellent, so don't be disappointed. Should I open the fridge? What do you think? Caviar is so shiny and minuscule, isn't it? I'm drooling already. I'll open a bottle of white, too. Oh, but do you like caviar? If you do, you can nod. Oh, not really? Why not? It's so good. You don't like it because it looks like ovaries? Or because it's creepy to see all the little black eggs clustered together? I don't think you understood what I said. You can't be so picky when you're a cook. Don't you want to be the best cook you can be? In such a perfect kitchen, too. Too bad, even if you don't like it. We'll eat this tonight.*

*Se-yeon, did you know that a female sturgeon with eggs is as valuable as gold? When you harvest eggs from a sturgeon you hit the softest part of its head to stun it. And then quickly with a flat sharp knife you pull out the egg sac from the body. Then an expert wearing a white coat and white gloves receives the large egg sac covered in membrane as if it's a baby. Because it's so expensive. The stunned sturgeon dies without knowing any better and the eggs are harvested in a perfect state. If the sturgeon is injured or scared or stressed the caviar doesn't taste good. Adrenalin pumps through so the eggs die or smell bad. So the perfect caviar has to be taken from a happy living sturgeon. This here is the most expensive caviar, which was harvested correctly. What do you think now? You're hungry, right? You want to eat it, right? I'm cutting this bread into thin slices like this and I'm going to toast it lightly with butter. And then I'm going to top it with a teaspoon of caviar and eat it. Se-yeon, you know you have to eat caviar by putting it in your mouth and popping it lightly with your tongue?*

*Water? Do you want more? Oh, you must be so thirsty. I'll give you warm water this time. Cold water is so fleeting. You know what'll happen if you yell, right? I always keep a promise. You keep the promise you made with me, okay? What is it? Is the water too hot? Don't worry. Once it goes past the tongue there won't be any damage to your throat or stomach. The tongue is the most heat-sensitive place on the body. So just drink it. If you shake your head like that the water keeps spilling. Just drink it all up. Instead of bothering me again for more water. Let me see, open your mouth. I guess it really was hot, your tongue is all red. But it's still healthy pink like a flamingo's tongue, and your taste buds are standing at attention too. Everything about you is so pretty! You must be so happy that you're beautiful and can get whatever you want. But looking at you drooling like that is kind of disgusting and sad. I hope he's never seen you make that expression. Do you know why Hemingway ate oysters at every meal? It's because he was feeling so empty. So empty, so he would slurp down oysters. That never happens to you, right?*

*You have something I want. I want you to give it to me. It doesn't matter now, but you've taken things from me.*

*Why are your legs trembling like that? Your legs are so long and gorgeous, like a flamingo's. Are you nervous? Don't be, you're getting sweaty and damp. You forgot what I told you about how to harvest the perfect caviar? What's that expression on your face? Is it shame? Or fear? You can't show that kind of emotion on your face. I want you to be more comfortable. I wonder what it felt like when those legs were wrapped around him in my kitchen.*

*Tongue is the tastiest part of the whale and apparently it's the same for a flamingo. I haven't tried one yet. It's so delicious that a Roman wrote about a flamingo, something like, My pink feathers gave me my name but gastronomes gave my tongue a reputation. There's something very strange about the tongue. It seems perfect but superficial. But what comes out of the mouth comes from the heart, right? So if you promise something, you have to keep it. That's what I want from you. The thing in your cavernous mouth, that.*

# CHAPTER 32

O N FRIDAYS, patients participating in family therapy sessions write a short autobiographical piece and read it aloud. Usually it revolves around their childhoods or family history or the reasons they started to rely on alcohol—revealing intimate details of the patient. Uncle participated in other activities but never went to these meetings until today. I study Uncle's face as he stands in front of strangers and reads his autobiography, condensed into two pieces of paper. I see fear, hesitation, sadness, and joy flitting across his face. What's changed with Uncle? If Uncle was starting to rehabilitate in June, in July he's reached the level of social adaptation. The third and last step. Some changes happen from the outside but some apparently occur from the inside. I wonder if the question he asked himself when he had the urge to drink was the catalyst for the change. Because asking yourself a question, a fundamental, unanswerable question, requires strong will and courage.

After the therapy session, we sit on a bench in the garden as always. Uncle has his hands linked behind his head, looking somewhere far away. Today may have been the first time he spoke about his wife in front of others.

"This flower, it looks like a cosmos," I remark, pointing at a golden-yellow daisy in the flowerbed, a strong saturated sprinkling of saffron.

"I never knew yellow was that beautiful," Uncle says in an embarrassed tone, frowning.

"Have you decided to forget her?" Is it because of the flower? The question I didn't want to ask pops out.

"Do you think that's what it is?"

"I don't know, I couldn't tell."

"How could I forget that person?"

That person. I try it after him, slowly.

"I'm just keeping her buried," he continues. "That's the only way I can move on. Because I don't think she would want me to live like this."

"Do you think love is like basil, Uncle?"

"What are you talking about?"

"I heard of a woman who couldn't let go of her dead lover's body. So she cut off his head and buried it in a plot under basil. She watered it with her tears but she died, unable to mend her broken heart. And from there bigger and fresher and more fragrant basil grew and people came from far away to look at it. So a woman loves a man, the man dies, the woman goes crazy, tears fall, plants grow—do you think it all boils down to that?"

"Not all love turns into that."

"I don't know what's love and what's true."

"What I'm saying is, not all true love makes you lose your calm like that. It's lunacy."

"Lunacy means there's an intense power, though."

Uncle is silent.

"Love is intense, Uncle."

"Yeah, maybe."

"Basil makes the heart dizzy, too. So you can't eat too much at once."

Uncle glances at me and smiles bitterly. "I don't know what went wrong."

I hang my head. "Why did we end up like this?"

"I don't know."

"Uncle, I don't understand it. We grew up peacefully eating apples and pears, raised by Grandmother, the best person in the world. But why did we both fail like this?"

"What do you think you've failed at? Love?"

I don't speak.

"You haven't failed at everything. It could be a small mistake, not a complete failure."

"It's the same thing."

"Remember when we put a watermelon in the freezer to chill and forgot about it until the next day? We broke into it to throw it away because it was frozen solid, and remember how the ice crystals glistened, enough to make it starry in front of our eyes? It was amazing. If it wasn't through a mistake we would never have seen such a thing."

I remember. The sparkling, starlike ice crystals that made us cry out in amazement.

"And you haven't failed. You're always comforted by cooking."

I'm quiet.

"Not everyone can be like that."

"When did you become so sweet? It's weird, Uncle."

". . . Because I'm scared."

"What?"

"Of starting all over again."

We're silent for a moment.

"Uncle."

"Yeah?"

"I don't think I'll be here when the cosmos bloom."

"What are you talking about?"

"I want to come up with a new way of cooking, from a peaceful and safe place, and not worry. Here, no matter what I make and eat I only feel sadness. I just want to be somewhere else."

"Are you tired, or are you looking for something new?"

"Both."

Uncle doesn't tell me not to go or to have a good trip. He doesn't ask when I'll be back. As if he knows I'm blatantly lying. *It's not like that, Uncle. Why do people feel love and hate toward the most fundamental things? Why do I always feel sorrow even when I eat something delicious?*

"I want to eat something made by your grandmother," Uncle says, stretching.

"Me too."

"You'll make it for me when you come back, right?" Uncle turns his head to look into my eyes.

*Of course.* I nod. "Do you know what my favorite smell is?"

"What?"

"The smell of someone cooking for me."

"Yeah, I think that's the same for me, too."

"Next time I think Mun-ju will be coming instead of me. That's okay, right? And the salt you gave me, I think I'll take it with me."

"Okay."

"But do you still need the washcloth?" I ask, narrowing my eyes mischievously.

"No, I'll be leaving here soon." Uncle gets up with me.

Farewells are always difficult. You can't laugh and you can't cry. It was the same way when Grandmother passed away. It was the same way when he left and when Paulie died. At the entrance to the hospital, Uncle kisses the top of my head. Then he says, Don't forget that cooking is the one thing you can do with your two hands. That you can push yourself up from the ground with those hands.

As I walk away, I think of the question that Uncle asked himself that changed him and wonder what question I need to ask myself. If I couldn't do it now, what would happen? If I didn't leave now, what would happen? If I don't talk about it now, what would happen?

These questions aren't right for me at this moment. What I have to do now is what I already decided to do. There's no reason to hesitate. You can't understand everything about love or force someone to get it completely. I won't ever be able to break free from this love, even if right now I think it's what I need to do. If I were a fish I wouldn't be able to think of myself as a separate being from water. Don't hesitate, I encourage myself in a loud voice. I know that a train with flashing red lights is rushing toward me at full speed, sounding its horn. And that it will eventually overtake me.

# CHAPTER 33

*I TELL HER THE FABLE of the tettorwort—you put it by the head of a sick person. If he's going to get better he'll shed tears and if he's going to die he'll sing. And I put a bundle of tetterwort with orange blossoms by her head.*

We have to wait and see, but I think it was the right choice to select B and D. For a while we trained our eyes on them, on the ones we hadn't wanted to hire. Thankfully B had the qualities D lacked—the basic, simple techniques and practicality—and D had a more vivid imagination. They knew how to share their talents, owning them together. Even better was that they were both conscientious. Before, I used to think of cooks as being either technicians or artists. I might have categorized Chef as an artist, waiting for inspiration, wondering how his food will set off fireworks. And I'm awkwardly straddling the two.

As I watch B and D, I start to think that all cooks might be craftsmen. Mastering the techniques and pursuing new ideas and having pride in their expertise and being happy to satisfy customers. The important thing is not whether a cook is a technician or an artist but whether he leaves the kitchen or not. A great chef never leaves the kitchen. After Chef became owner, the time he spent in the kitchen remained the same even though it became more important to serve clients than to cook. Still, the cook I prefer is B. Although D isn't too bad, he is a little cocky. B blends in. For a chaotic, narrow kitchen, the person who doesn't stand out is the useful one, although perhaps not so much in other situations.

Over the last thirteen years, Chef saw that I had finally become a useful cook, although I didn't stand out at first. And if he watches me a little carefully now, he must know what I want. I put on his desk the new, still unused kitchen towel I received that day in February when I came back to work and the white envelope I bought for the resignation letter I never wrote when I quit four years ago. Sometimes you need formality. Chef takes the envelope without saying a word. He's standoffish, as if he knew this would happen, disappointing me a little. Like a monk, he doesn't talk when he eats and doesn't smile easily and is stern. He knows as soon as meat touches his lips whether it was aged for a day or a week, and he sometimes makes a plate of tortellini for staff who have fallen in love, and on his shoulder and the back of his hand he has a tattoo shaped like a hurricane like the Maori, and if he gets into a fight he wouldn't be easily knocked down and would probably still be standing for the last round. Chef believes that you shouldn't be surprised under any circumstance. The man who led me into the world of cooking—can he really see through me, like through water? Does he know what I'm thinking?

*I pry open her mouth while she is unconscious from the clove and pull at her tongue. Muscular, covered in membrane, sprouting from under the roof of her mouth near the jawbone, the tongue feels slippery and solid. I stretch out the muscle used when sticking out the tongue, the one that attaches the tongue to the jaw. It's not as long as I thought it would be. If I cut the muscle along the jawline and pull open the glands under the chin, then I think I can cut the base of the tongue.*

*To cook you have to understand the anatomy of your ingredients. Especially for a meat dish. When you kill an animal, it's best to hit it over the head. Because that makes the meat more tender. History shows that food lovers did not stop at anything if it pertained to taste. They kicked a pregnant sow until she was dead so the milk would mix with the fetus, then cut out the fetus and put it on the table. They plucked the feathers of a goose and buttered it and, to make sure it didn't die of thirst, gave it a platter of water as it was roasted alive. When the goose leapt about madly and started to stagger, they cut into it and ate it up before it was dead. To obtain the best beef they grabbed the scrotum of a young calf, stretched it out, and cut it off in one swipe. When they butchered the calf they sprinkled water on its head, then grabbed it and shook it. They even killed trout in a sealed glass bottle, watching the fish jump around, trying to live, shiver, and slowly die, its color losing luster, and they felt excitement before even tasting it. Back in the day people thought food that died violently enhanced the taste and was good for the health. Now it's been proven that a painless, calm butchering technique is better for the taste.*

*Careful not to nudge her too hard, I cautiously move her body so she's lying on her back with her arms by her sides. All pictures of human bodies in the book are in this position. The typical dissection pose. You can taste even if you don't have a tongue or a frenum. People who were born without tongues or whose tongues were cut off can still taste because taste buds are dispersed throughout the insides of their cheeks. The painful thing about not having a tongue is not that you can't taste anything but that it's painful when you swallow. Especially extremely sour or bitter food, which causes unbearable pain. I place a few kernels of sea salt on her tongue and close her mouth.*

He's looking at my recipe quietly. I streamlined it and switched up a few ingredients. I feel myself getting nervous. Now I really don't have time to fix it. I worked on it and thought about it for a long time. If I can't do this, I don't know if I can make the other one down the road. He nods slowly as if to agree and puts down the paper. *The scent is going to be too strong. If you can get your hands on it you should use green pepper, not black.* I nod. Black and white pepper are harvested when the fruit is completely ripe, but green pepper is plucked just before it's ready, doused in salt water or vinegar, and flash frozen. It has a fresher, fruity scent, like a fig, so it works well in duck or beef dishes. This time, Chef doesn't ask whether I would use ox tongue. Instead he asks, Do you really want to make this dish? It's got such a persistent taste. I nod again. I think it's enough that the recipe is completed. I shake my head and ask to borrow his knife. *Because mine's so dull, I need a sharper and more flexible knife, Chef.* I feel him staring ferociously at my forehead.

Take it.

Chef takes a white envelope out of his pocket, much like the one I gave him, and sticks it out toward me. I look down at the airline logo that resembles the profile of a bird printed on the corner of the envelope and ask, Is there anything you'd like to eat? I don't have anything to give him or leave for him but I can make warm mushroom soup or spinach porridge in minutes. He laughs silently but it's loud in my head. I hang my head. *I don't think you can make it for me. What I want to eat is something made by the person who loves me.* I can't make him that. But if he wants something humble and simple like Grandmother's food, I can do that for him. But I don't say that. I don't say I'll make it for him next time, either. Because I may not be able to keep that promise. Instead I say, with a hint of annoyance in my voice, Chef, you always want dishes that don't exist. As if it's the biggest problem between us. When it's hot like this it's time to make a more sensual dish, he says. I ask him why the name of the restaurant is the number nine. Chef smiles ruefully. *Because it seems incomplete and complete at the same time.*

We sit across from each other silently for another ten minutes.

Chef gets up first. He's ready to part ways. I push my chair back and stand up too. If I were older I think I would want to be with a man who makes decisions for me. But now I can do it on my own. I hold out my hand. He doesn't take it. He comes around behind me and lifts his hand as if he would pat my shoulder but places it gently on the back of my neck. Is it his pointer or middle finger? It feels like a sun-warmed pebble is touching the bones of my neck. He runs that finger down my spine. I stand still. As he does that he's mumbling something. I don't really hear it but I keep nodding.

One minute. Or maybe twenty or thirty seconds. A short time, but it feels longer than any time we spent together and it's as if we're saying a long farewell. We say a farewell that isn't dotted with tears or laughter, that holds no wistful feelings. He turns around and goes into the kitchen and I push through the front doors and leave.

I wake up from my sleep. I hear through the smell of grass a thin and faint song, like weeping.

# CHAPTER 34

TONGUE WITH TRUFFLES

Serves one

*Ingredients:*
150 grams fresh red tongue
Leek
Onion
Carrots
Celery
Radish
Thyme
White wine
Water
Pinch of salt
Two spears asparagus
Truffles

*For the sauce:*
100 grams watercress
Garlic
Truffle oil
Lemon juice to taste
Whole green peppercorns

*Directions:*
1. In a large pot, boil leeks, onion, carrots, celery, radish, thyme, white wine, water, salt, and tongue for 30 minutes. The tongue will shrink when it is dropped in the boiling water.
2. Remove the tongue from the stock. When the tongue cools, cut off the membranes.
3. Preheat the oven to 400 degrees.
4. Place the tongue in the oven and bake for 15 minutes.
5. Cut the tongue into half-inch slices.
6. Snap off the ends of the asparagus and steam or sauté in olive oil in a hot pan.
7. In a bowl, mix together the ingredients for the sauce. Finely grind whole green peppercorns.
8. Pour the sauce on a plate and arrange the slices of tongue on top. Garnish with sliced truffles. Place the asparagus on the side.

*Suggestions:*
• Instead of baking the tongue in the oven, try pan-frying it in olive oil.
• If the scent of the sauce is too intense, you can replace the watercress with finely minced Italian parsley and garlic in a 3:2 ratio.
• If the tongue is not the freshest, you can add nutmeg to enhance its flavor.

# CHAPTER 35

I NO LONGER BELIEVE that the truffle symbolizes love. Love shatters with the rumbling of thunder, but thunder causes truffles to grow. Sure, both are hard to find. You harvest truffles, which can't be seen by the human eye, by following a trained sow with an excellent sense of smell. So it's closer to hunting. Truffles are black and round like a forgotten, burnt potato. Among food lovers, the truffle is considered precious, along with caviar and foie gras, exciting them with a whiff and giving them joy. The black diamond of the earth shatters more easily than glass, and it's hard to handle. Too much of it works as an aphrodisiac, like nutmeg or cloves. Even expert harvesters exercise extreme caution when harvesting, sliding a finger carefully into the ground. The truffle is difficult to work with unless you're an experienced, skilled cook; it is the subject of worship. Even though you can't see them and you can't tell for sure, you pile branches over the spots where you think they may grow to maintain the right humidity. You harvest them in October and November and they are reborn in the next autumn rain. Every time I have a chance to eat truffles I wonder whether they are so treasured not because of their unique taste and scent of aged mud, but because you can't find them easily and they're impossible to farm. Truffles are always a part of the priciest dishes. I take out the truffle I obtained through Chef in May, which I sealed in a bottle in olive oil. Perfection is the key to sublime taste.

The touched expression on his face is probably because of the truffle. His eyes sparkle and his skin—the scalpel's first point of contact if he were to be dissected—is taut and excited, anticipating the feast. And he asks again, as if to be reassured, "So this dinner is really the last time, right?"

I tell him that I won't be contacting him again. After seven persistent calls he finally agreed and came to the house today. I put down the truffle and turn toward him. He used to be the person to whom I wanted to give my best. He used to be the person who made me feel as if I were looking at a better version of myself. The last thing I can give him is tonight's feast.

I turn up the corners of my mouth and smile. "Of course. I won't even call anymore. I keep my promises."

"Okay . . . thanks."

"You're thanking me already before you've eaten? But what's happened with Se-yeon?"

"Hmm?"

"I heard from Mun-ju. Se-yeon disappeared without a word?"

"Oh, no, it's not like that."

"What happened?"

"She said she wanted to rest a bit. Because when the cooking class opens she won't have that kind of time."

"Oh . . . so you heard from her?"

"Yeah, a few days ago."

"Where is she?"

"Why are you so curious? You don't even like her."

"No, that's not true."

"Really?"

"Yeah. Because of her I realized how much I treasure you."

"That's a little awkward to hear."

"So when's she coming back?"

"Soon."

"Soon?"

"Yeah."

"I'm sure she'll come back soon. Like nothing's happened." He changes the subject. "But you look happy."

"Oh, maybe because of my dream."

"Dream?"

"Yeah, I had a dream about a beakfish."

"Beakfish?"

"The Mediterranean fish with a golden crescent on its forehead. It's really rare to catch that fish."

"So you dreamed of a rare fish. I guess something good is going to happen to you."

I'm standing in the kitchen wearing chef's whites and my heels with pearls in the soles. Once, my favorite pastime was to stand in this open kitchen and make dinner, the person I love sitting in front of me. Why does everything feel so far away, as if it will never happen again? And why isn't it happening again? I look at him over the chopping block. *Seok-ju, I'm glad that after this dinner my heart can leave you, go far away, gradually.* I dip my hot fingertips in ice water. "I'm going to Italy tomorrow."

"Oh, really?" He can't hide his relief. *Both of you are the same—you are not careful.* I open the fridge and take out the tongue that I aged after cleaning off the tendons and tattered muscles. I have to concentrate my cold fingertips on this deep red tongue. I wrap my palm around the knife. It feels good. The knife under my full control. This feeling is why I handle meat. I pour him another glass of champagne as an aperitif.

And I whisper sweetly, "Don't get drunk yet. I'm going to make you such a good meal that it's going to melt your tongue."

He lets his guard down because of his expectations for the meal, or maybe because I won't be here tomorrow. If one person has changed and the other hasn't, their former love becomes pathetic and stagnant and cruel. It's better not to talk about the old times. But today may really be the last time that we sit across from each other in our kitchen and eat. Instead of feeling miserable, I feel sentimental.

"Do you remember that time?" I ask.

"What time?"

"When you regained consciousness."

"Oh, yeah."

"It was six months later."

". . . Yeah."

"I still remember what you said when you opened your eyes." He's quiet.

"You grabbed my hand and squeezed it."

"Is dinner almost ready?"

"You told me we shouldn't be apart anymore, remember? That you were afraid of not seeing me again. That even though you were unconscious, it was so real and painful. So you just kept thinking, this is a dream, a dream, I'm just dreaming."

". . . You said you wouldn't do this. You told me it was only dinner."

"When you were unconscious it wasn't that hard. Even though the guy who caused the accident died, I knew you would wake up. You had to wake up, for me."

"If you keep doing this, I'm leaving."

"I'm making dinner right now. Just wait. It's almost done. If you just leave now I might keep calling and bothering you, and not leave and stay here. That's not what you want, is it?"

He's silent.

"So just be quiet and stay."

"What's the main course today?"

"Of course it's meat, it's what you like. But today I cut it a little thinner."

". . . Why?"

"Do you know why people started cooking sliced meat?"

He's quiet.

"Because it became uncivilized to put an entire animal on the table. You want to eat meat but you feel uneasy. So they started to slice it smaller. And you can keep distance from the animal being eaten. But isn't it kind of funny? It's not like it changes the nature of it."

"I'm hungry. Is it ready yet?"

"You just want to leave here as soon as possible."

"No, it's just because I want to eat. Something smells so great."

"I think it was when you were recovering from the accident. We were taking a walk and you said, I'm the happiest right in this moment. You stroked Paulie with one hand and grabbed my hand with the other. I was so happy that tears sprang to my eyes. I was so happy that you had come to and that you were happy. Unbelievably happy. And I smelled bursting thyme. I felt that delicate herb exploding and spreading like popcorn."

"Did you ask me to come for this?"

"No, no. It's almost ready. I'll give you soup first."

He sits down again, resigned. I place a tart green summer apple that I'd frozen after scooping out the inside, frosty, on the table. Inside is a cold soup made with apple, butter, sugar, broth. It would go down his throat sweetly and softly. I chose this soup because I thought it would go best with the strong, tough tongue. He takes a spoonful to his mouth and his face blooms. "It's cold and sweet and silky. I bet the world's first apple tasted like this."

"Adam and Eve made love after eating an apple."

"What?"

*The apple that was placed in her armpit.* For people with a sensitive sense of taste and a certain sensuality, the most amazing scent is that of their lover's sweat. He laps up every last drop of the soup, scraping the bottom of the apple with his spoon. *Her smell will keep him relaxed.* At least until this meal is finished.

"Now it's time for salad." I serve a salad of arugula and grapefruit. Then it will be time for the main course. I have to gradually awaken his senses. The sweet-and-sour grapefruit and bitter arugula would gently waft past the bumpy taste buds like a spring breeze.

"Simple, and you can taste nature."

"Good. I'll get you a different wine. It's time for the main course."

I bring out two tall Riedel wineglasses, shaped like tulips about to bloom. The wine I got for tonight's meal is Barolo Zonchera. It goes especially well with flavorful meat dishes. The wine he ordered on his first visit to Nove, when I leaned on the pass to steal glances at him, while he was immersed in eating my steak.

I pour a glass of the Barolo for myself. I place the tongue in the middle of a large white plate and top it with three slivers of truffle, and next to it I place fresh oven-roasted asparagus in a V shape. The deep brown tongue, intense gray truffle, and mellow green asparagus clustered on the white plate impart trust before they're tasted. *The reason chimpanzees eat each other's brains is that their souls are in them. Our souls live here. In this tongue. Now it's your turn to tell me what it tastes like.*

I dim the kitchen lights.

I take a white cloth trimmed with lace from a cabinet.

I pick up the plate carefully with both hands and place it on the table.

"Your favorite poet, Baudelaire, said, Be always drunk on wine, or poetry, or virtue."

His face splits into a smile upon seeing the plate. "So you're saying, get drunk on virtue!"

"Right. Try it." I slip the white cloth over his head. *This is what they did when eating ortolan. When they chewed on the bird's rib cage and wings, bones and innards, in the dark with a cloth over their heads, they were able to relive the bird's entire life. They really understood taste, didn't they?*

He takes up the fork and knife obediently. Slices of tongue fan out in perfect symmetry on the sauce of garlic, peppercorn, truffle oil, lemon, and watercress. He pierces the middle piece, the biggest, the one with the clearest shape. Immobile, I watch him put it into his mouth and close his lips and move his chin slowly, chewing. A smile spreads across his face.

"How is it?"

"There's something really tough about it, but it has a really good texture. It even feels crisp under my teeth, like very hard vegetables. Is this really beef?"

"Of course, of course," I nod vigorously.

He puts another bite in his mouth and chews. "How can it taste like this? It's so good."

"There's something special in my recipe, you know."

"I feel a power in my mouth like two strongmen are competing against each other. Not just a fight that splatters blood but something that creates harmony, like a fight of taste."

"Really?"

"Yeah. The taste is so alive—it's leaping around on my tongue."

You can't fool taste. His pupils are starting to dilate. He chews carefully and swallows, one morsel after another. As if he's enveloped in a holy light, his face becomes flushed and sweat dots his forehead. He's sinking into my new dish. I hear from far away the patter of cats walking across the yard and raindrops falling into the drain. The feast has to be the last thing of the day. In quiet and intimacy like this. Like travelers who want to get to the same destination together. I feel the ground swaying peacefully. I'm standing on water. Dizziness sweeps across me. I pause from stirring the watermelon sherbet that's for dessert and whisper in his ear, "Should we kiss just one time? Just once?" This is the end.

His eyes betray wariness. I grab his right wrist, the one holding the fork.

"Okay, because you're truly a great cook. But this really is it."

We approach each other slowly and our lips touch, fluttering, a resting of my face on a frost-covered winter window. Not too hot or close or passionate. Like a shy first kiss, tentative and soft.

I open my eyes and look into his. One man and one woman. Like every love story, there are happy times if you look back. And the first moment of seduction that drew us in. But now it's time to go back to our places. To feel more and to remember more. We have returned to our first shared moment. But maybe we are now different trees. Trees that can only drink in different musical notes. Everything starts to die as soon as it's born. Some things thrive and others decline while some are reborn and others float away. The thing that lives, gradually changes. It's not important to go somewhere but it's crucial that we're moving. In the dark I quickly wipe away a tear with the back of my hand and with his fork I spear a piece of tongue and gently push it between his red lips.

# A NOTE ON THE AUTHOR

Kyung Ran Jo was born in Seoul, South Korea, in 1969. She earned a degree in creative writing from Seoul Institute of the Arts and has participated in the University of Iowa's renowned International Writing Program. Since her fiction debut at age twenty-eight, she has earned numerous literary awards including the Today's Young Artist Prize from the South Korean Ministry of Culture and Tourism and the Dong-in Literary Award for her newest short-story collection, *I Bought Balloons. Tongue,* an immediate bestseller in South Korea, is her first novel to be translated into English.